As RV enters sophomore year, his friendships and relationships create more questions than answers. RV still cares for Bobby, but Bobby seems a different, more distant person. RV's best friend Carole is distracted by the ups and downs in her relationships with her French boyfriends, while RV's new friend Mark is more focused on his family's troubles. School is a mixed bag. RV enjoys the Spanish club he has joined, which is run by his beautiful Spanish teacher, Señorita Sanchez. But he struggles with other subjects and annoying teachers and always has to watch out for the school bullies who seem to know how to stay under the detention radar.

As always, RV's former teacher and mentor, Mr. Aniso, is there for advice, especially when near-tragedy strikes and RV needs Mr. Aniso's counsel to stay strong and provide help where it's needed most.

WHY CAN'T RELATIONSHIPS BE LIKE PIZZA?

The Pizza Chronicles, Book Three

Andy V. Roamer

A NineStar Press Publication

www.ninestarpress.com

Why Can't Relationships Be Like Pizza?

Printed in the USA

ISBN: 978-1-64890-171-3

First Edition, February, 2021

Also available in eBook, ISBN: 978-1-64890-170-6

WARNING:
This book contains homophobic slurs.

To Nancy, thanks for your support, for helping Rimas heal, and for taking care of Mom.

Chapter One

What's Up with My Relationships?

I thought sophomore year would be easier. I got through freshman year okay, even got an award for good grades and good behavior. Yeah, I'm such an angel. It'll take a long time to live that down. Whalen is in my homeroom again. Hope he's over drawing pictures of his classmates, especially me. If he only knew the real me, maybe he wouldn't have drawn that halo over my head.

Anyway, sophomore year sure isn't starting out any easier. I can already tell my Chemistry class is going to be no picnic. I'm a right-brain guy, creative and nerdy, ha ha, not analytical and nerdy. And too bad I don't have Mr. Aniso for Latin class this year. It would be great reading *Julius Caesar* with him, wouldn't it? Better than having Latin with Miss Wagstaff. Reminds me of a librarian crossed with some of our nuns in grammar school. She's tall and skinny with tight curly hair and these round granny glasses that make her eyes look huge. She never smiles, and when she gets mad, her eyes get bigger behind those glasses, her arms fly around, and she starts to screech like one of those scary prehistoric birds. Oh, for the days of Mr. Aniso.

And this year's Math teacher, Mr. Felucci, never smiles either. He's strict too. Reminds me of a mean, fat army sergeant who likes to put you on the spot in class. Not fun for my right-sided brain.

At least there's Señorita Sánchez, our Spanish teacher. She's from Spain and so gorgeous, even I might start to have fantasies about her. She's tough, too, but nice about it. Doesn't make us feel bad if we get something wrong.

So, school's not all bad, right? I guess not. But it's my life that's—what?—kind of somewhere out there in some crazy zone, not exactly where I want it to be. Especially where my friends are concerned. Most importantly, Bobby. I still think we're close, aren't we? We did have that nice talk in our favorite place in the woods, where he apologized and said he still cared about me. I'm so happy for him. He was so excited about making the varsity football team.

But guess what? I haven't seen him since then. Not alone anyway. He's not in any of my classes. Oh, I see him in the corridors at school, where he's nice to me, like he's nice to everybody. That's what makes him so great. Mr. Nice Guy, despite being a jock and making the varsity football team. He could be so full of himself, though he's not. He's just busy with school and practice. Always practice. So, friends have to take second place. Is that how it works?

And then Carole, my wonderful Carole. I thought when she got back from Paris, we'd be getting together a lot. But I've only seen her once. All she talked about was François. A gorgeous French guy she met over there. François this, François that. She barely asked me about my summer.

Well, okay. She's got a huge crush. People who get crushes are a little off the wall, especially if that crush is on someone from a foreign country. The foreign person seems so exotic and all that. So, you have to give them some space, right? At least through the end of the year. Carole told me François and his family were coming to Boston to visit relatives for the holidays.

Then there's my wonderful family. I haven't known whether they're coming or going for a long time, so it's no use complaining about them. At least Mom and Dad got their citizenship, so that should settle things down for a bit. Mom can concentrate on her jewelry business, and Dad still has his job. Even if he loses his job, which he says can happen anytime, now that he's a citizen it should be easier for him to find another job, right? Though to hear Dad talk about it, there are enough undocumented immigrants in the construction business, it's just not out in the open. So why did we spend so much time studying that booklet with all those questions? He should be happy he passed the test. But he's still complaining, now about all those undocumented guys. I wish he could be happy for a change.

Like Ray. What? My little brother happy? Yeah, there's been a change in him in the last few weeks. He sits at the dinner table, smiling sometimes. Offers to pass the potatoes. If Dad tells him to put away his phone, he does it without arguing. Doesn't even say anything smart-alecky back in English. Almost acts like the good obedient son of immigrants his parents want him to be. Really? Ray talking Lith-speak? *"Taip." "Ačiū." "Ar galiu daugiau bulvių?"* "Yes." "Thank you." "May I have more potatoes?" How long is that going to last?

Like I said, with my family, I never know if they're coming or going or running around in crazy circles.

Well, at least there's Joe's Pizza. Always Joe's. One thing I can count on. Even though it looks like Bobby's football teammates have discovered it, Joe's Pizza is still a good place to come and chill out. Maybe I don't need to find another place. How could I ever leave Joe's? And one good thing about football practice. It's not just Bobby who's so busy. All those guys are busy after school practicing. So, they haven't been coming here much. It looks like I'll still be able to come and have my slice in peace, at least until football season ends.

So, RV, just settle down and start your homework. You can always write more in your diary after your three or four hours of hitting the books. Who am I kidding? I'll be so tired then, I'll be sick of looking at the computer screen. I'll just want to go to bed. That's what I get for being smart and going to Boston Latin School.

Am I smart? There are a lot of smart kids here, so I don't feel so smart. It takes a lot of work just to keep up.

But I wouldn't be happier being dumb, would I? No. How about just kind of average? Not that either.

So here I come, sophomore year! You're not going to get me down, even if I have no idea where I fit in or what you have in store for me!

*

I'm not wrong about Bobby. I wish were, but I do get the sense he's avoiding me. Well, maybe not avoiding me exactly, but I'm not as important to him as I thought I was.

I texted him the other day just to say hi and see how he was doing. He was friendly and all that, but when I asked if we could get together again this week, he put me off, telling me practice was taking all his time. And it's not the first time the conversation went like that.

I get that part. I know he's really excited about being on the varsity football team. And nervous, too, wanting to show everyone he deserves to be on the team. That he's not just a token sophomore with all those juniors and seniors. Or a token black athlete. He hates being a token of any kind.So, he's working extra hard. I really do get that.

But that's not what I'm complaining about. Carole was off doing something else, too, so I took myself to Joe's for a slice. I don't mind going there alone. I take a book or some homework and relax. Joe is always very friendly to me. If he's not too busy, he'll tell me about the business and ask me how I'm doing. It's fun to talk to him.

Joe tells me what he goes through running the business. Who knew there was so much involved owning a little pizza joint? As for me, I try not to complain too much, so I usually just say "I'm fine." Joe nods and says, "Keep it that way, RV." And then sometimes, he even gives me a slice for free, wanting me to try one of the new crazy pizza combinations he's working out. I've become his taste tester, LOL. It's great when I like something, like the Super Jalapeño, but not when it's something like the slice with all those disgusting anchovies.

Today I just ordered a regular cheese slice and sat down in a booth, ready to go over some reading for Chemistry class. But who should walk in but Bobby with a couple of his teammates?

"Hey, RV. How you doin'?" he said, looking cheerful and relaxed.

"Hey, Bobby," I answered. I'm sure I sounded cheerful, too, since I'm always glad to see him. But then I remembered something. "Don't you have practice this afternoon?"

Bobby shook his head. "Nope. Practice is cancelled. Coach said something came up with his family, and the assistant coach can't make it either."

Bobby's teammates ordered slices and sat down at a nearby booth. "C'mon, join us," Bobby said.

I hesitated for a second and then shook my head. "Ah, thanks, but I really have to study. Have my first Chemistry quiz tomorrow, and these stupid equations still don't make sense to me."

"Are you sure?" Bobby asked, though he was already making his way over to the booth where his teammates were sitting.

"Yeah, I'm sure. Thanks again. If I'm finished, maybe I can come over then," I added, though I knew that was a lie. If by some miracle I finally figured out all those equations, it would take so long that Bobby and his teammates would be long gone.

So, I put my head down and tried to concentrate on my homework. But I couldn't help overhearing Bobby and his teammates. They talked about practice routines, other teams they would be playing against this fall, other players, and what they liked or didn't like about their coaches. I could make out Bobby's voice among the others, laughing and adding his opinion.

I did glance up a couple of times, not being able to stop myself. Bobby was sitting facing me, so I could see how happy he was. No, not just happy. What's the word I'm looking for? He was glowing, looking like he'd never been happier. Like that's where he belonged. Forever. With his teammates, in the world of football, not with me. I don't think I existed for him at that point. He certainly never looked my way or gave any indication he was thinking about me.

He had promised me the last time we sat in the woods that the gay stuff wouldn't come between us. That he didn't care if people saw me with Mr. Aniso, who doesn't particularly try hard to hide his sexuality. Not that he could successfully since he's so swishy. I thought

Bobby was feeling better about his own gay feelings too. That I still mattered a lot to him. And he wanted to be with me. That he *cared*. It's not the feeling I get since sophomore year started.

Like today. If practice was cancelled, he could have called me up. Makes me wonder how many other times Bobby did have some free time but didn't call me.

I'm not being unreasonable, am I? I don't come on too strong, do I? I don't act gay, whatever that means. And it's not like I have figured everything out. I have more questions than anything else. Sometimes I even wonder if I really am gay. Since Bobby has some of the same questions, you would think he'd want to spend more time with me.

I was thinking about all those things sitting in that booth. It was impossible to concentrate anymore. I gathered up my stuff even though those equations still didn't make much more sense to me. It was time to leave. I got up and did walk up to Bobby and his teammates and said goodbye. Everybody was friendly enough, but I still felt awkward, knowing I don't belong in their world. And Bobby didn't act any differently from his teammates or say anything that indicated we were friends or that he wanted to see me later.

So, after a few more awkward moments, I turned around and left Joe's.

And here I sit now, in front of my computer, for the zillionth time, trying to figure out my life. Does it ever change or get easier? Mr. Aniso keeps assuring me it does, but sometimes I wonder. Maybe he's just saying that to make me feel better. After all, when we're talking, I sometimes see the sadness that comes over his face. So, he's got stuff going on his life too. He did seem happy when he introduced me to his new friend, Ben. Hope it lasts. For his sake. And mine.

*

I was sitting there at dinner with my family. In some ways it was the usual dinner. Mom baked a chicken, which I thought tasted pretty good. Dad complained, saying he was getting sick of chicken. Mom told him with the money we had budgeted for food, we couldn't afford steak every night. Dad grumbled a bit, but then kept quiet.

And Ray shrugged. Like I said, my little brother's changed. Normally he would be taking out his phone and listening to some song or other until Dad told him to put it away. But lately Ray's just been sitting quietly, eating his meal, not complaining, and even giving Mom a compliment or two. Don't know what's gotten into him, but I guess it's good. As long as the pot he was smoking this summer hasn't gone to his brain. I still haven't said anything to Mom and Dad about it. Am I a coward or a loyal brother?

Mom and Dad started talking about work. Mom's happy with her part-time job at Neiman Marcus and the online jewelry business she's starting that she says will give us a little extra much-needed income. Money. Is it always about money? Dad still worries about his job, but now that he's a full-fledged citizen he admits he's a little less scared. But he says construction jobs are not easy to get these days, so gives us his old spiel about money not growing on trees. (Spiel. Wonder where that word comes from? Dad has a lot of spiels. Stories about the Old Country, his new country, and how we kids don't appreciate what we have here.)

Well, that's one thing that hasn't changed. Two things. Dad's complaining and my being interested in words. So, I'm still a nerd. I wonder if a sophomore nerd is better than a freshman one, ha ha.

After Mom and Dad finished talking about their jobs and money, Dad started talking about someone at work who he's becoming friendly with. Dad said he's a nice guy and maybe he'd like to invite him over sometime. And then suddenly I heard the word "gay." I snapped to attention and tried to hide it by looking down at my food and concentrating on eating. But there was the word again. Dad was saying rumors were going around that the guy might be "that way." Mom was nodding, saying she wasn't surprised, there were a lot of gays in every job, certainly working with her at Neiman Marcus.

I looked up. Dad was shrugging, looking a little puzzled. He was saying the guy seemed nice and normal.

Ray piped up, *"O, kas yra normal?"* "What's normal?"

Both Mom and Dad turned to him.

He continued, *"Aš turiu draugę, kuri yra bisexual."* "I have a female friend who is bisexual."

Mom looked surprised.

Dad looked annoyed, reminding Ray he was thirteen years old, and what did he know about bisexuals.

I guess the old Ray is still there somewhere because he wasn't intimidated at all. He continued talking, telling Dad everyone knew about bisexuals. They had sex with both men and women and there were more of them around than people realized.

Mom told him she preferred that he think more about homework than bisexuals.

They continued talking about the subject while I sat there, feeling myself blush. And how would they react if they knew about me? Why couldn't I be like Ray, and add my two cents to the conversation? "Oh, yeah, Mom, Dad. I've thought about being bisexual sometimes too. But I think I'm more gay than bisexual."

I glanced over at them. Talking about a stranger was one thing, but how would they react if it was their son? Mom might be okay, after a while. But Dad? He didn't have the angry look he's had in the past when the subject of gays had come up. Maybe he was changing. Or maybe because he was talking about a person he liked, he couldn't be angry. Maybe that's why he looked more confused than anything else. Still, it doesn't take much to make Dad angry. I've seen it in the past, so it's better not to take chances. And when he gets really angry, well, I don't want to think about that now.

Everyone dropped the subject when Mom brought out some dessert. But I'm still thinking about it now I'm up in my room alone. Would I like to tell Mom and Dad what's going on inside me? I suppose so. I don't like having this thing come between us. Maybe they'd react better than I give them credit for. But it feels so private. Like it's mine and mine alone. Why is that? Do they deserve to know? At what point? When I'm more sure about things? Ha! At the rate I'm going, that might take years.

So, another relationship that's confusing me. Man, I better start on my homework. As much as that's a pain, it's much easier dealing with homework than with all these questions about myself and all these people in my life.

Chapter Two

Sophomore Slump

"Hola, Señor RV. ¿Cómo está usted?"

"Bien, Señora Sánchez."

"Señor RV. Soy Señorita, no Señora Sánchez."

"Ah, si. Perdóneme, Señorita Sánchez."

"Gracias, Señor RV. Soy la señorita porque no estoy casada. ¿No es así?"

Whew! Got a workout from Señorita Sánchez in Spanish class today. She gets mad when we call her Señora, keeps reminding us that we have to call her Miss because she's not married. I thought I knew that.

Maybe it's because she has this serious look about her, like she's a Señora. Hard to imagine her not married to some Spanish bigwig or rich businessman. She's pretty old, maybe thirty or forty, but has as much energy as someone our age, and you don't want to be caught asleep in her class. She's very pretty too. I'll have to ask Carole if all the women in Europe are so pretty, sexy even. Yeah, sexy. The guys all smile when she walks through the rows in class and make quiet jokes behind her back. Can't say I blame them. She walks with a little swing in her hips and wears interesting dresses and multicolored scarves.

"Glad she didn't call on me."

I nodded. "Yeah, lucky me," I whispered, frowning.

That was Mark, the guy sitting in front of me. We're getting friendly. He's a nice guy, pretty studious and quiet like me, so we have a lot in common. He lives in Roslindale, the next part of Boston over from us. He came to Latin School from eighth grade like me, not sixth grade, like most of the students. We're Bs, the students who came to Latin into ninth grade. The As are the ones who came into seventh grade. A little discrimination there? Why should we be called Bs? We're as good as the As.

So, we have that discrimination in common too. Maybe we'll become real friends. It would be nice to have another friend, since Bobby's so busy and Carole's off in her own world these days, thinking about her François.

"See you in the cafeteria?" Mark asked at the end of class, after Señorita Sánchez gave us another whopper of a Spanish article to decipher for homework.

"Sure," I agreed.

"I wish I were good in languages like you," Mark said, when lunchtime came, and we were eating our sandwiches.

"Well, maybe I have a little head start, given my background," I said. "But I still have to study hard. It's not like Lithuanian and Spanish are the same."

Mark knows about my background. That I'm a kid of immigrants from Eastern Europe. That I didn't learn to speak English until I went to kindergarten. That we speak the Mother Tongue, Lithuanian, at home. I keep reminding him that while knowing two languages has some advantages, it has some disadvantages too. Like not knowing which world I'm in sometimes.

Mark looked a little dejected today.

"What's the matter?" I asked him.

He shrugged. "I study hard too," he said. "But I still have trouble remembering all this Spanish. The last thing I need to do is flunk a class."

He complained about his parents putting pressure on him. I nodded in sympathy, telling him about my parents putting pressure on me.

"It's only September," I said, trying to reassure him, maybe myself too. "It's too early to think about flunking."

"I know," he said. "I have to learn to concentrate and not look at Señorita Sánchez's breasts."

"Her breasts?"

"Yeah. Haven't you noticed how big they are?"

I felt the old RV blush coming on. I had noticed them. They were big, but they hadn't distracted me too much, not like they distracted Mark apparently. Should I have been distracted? There were Bobby's words again, ringing in my ears. "Oh, RV. You're so innocent."

"Don't you think about them?"

"Huh?"

"Señorita Sánchez's breasts. Don't you think about them?" Mark asked.

"Well, I guess sometimes, yeah," I answered.

"I think about them a lot," Mark was saying. "The minute I try to do my Spanish homework, those breasts come into my mind. And then I think about how they would look naked. It's much easier than trying to conjugate or memorize the stupid *preterito imperfecto*." Mark looked at me. "Don't you think about women's breasts?"

"Ah, sure." I told him about the time I was going out with Carole and she used to show off her bras. "She wasn't naked," I said, "but that came pretty close."

Mark seemed impressed.

I sat there thinking about Bobby and the times we kissed. Did I dare tell Mark about that? How would he react to any talk about being gay? Or sex for that matter? Mark told me he comes from a very Christian, born-again family. I think he's a pretty conservative guy, so it didn't seem like a good idea to bring it up.

Mark was talking about the Spanish homework again. "So, will you help me, RV?" he was asking.

"Oh, ah, sure," I said, trying to focus on the conversation. "Maybe I can introduce you to my friend, Carole. She spent much of the summer in Paris. Some words in French are similar to Spanish, so maybe Carole can help us a little bit."

"Wow, Paris. I've never been out of the country."

"Me neither. Lucky Carole. It sounds like she had a great time."

"Yeah, who wouldn't?" said Mark. "If all the women look like Señorita Sánchez, man, I'd be going crazy."

We made some more jokes about Señorita Sánchez and European women. Then we went off to our next classes.

I had a little time off from concentrating the rest of the afternoon too. I was thinking about Mark. He seems like a nice guy, and I like him. And I do hope we become friends. But with his background, would he have any patience for anyone gay? Born-agains hate gays. Well, maybe not all of them, but enough of them. I've never heard Mark say anything about gays one way or another. No calling anyone faggot or anything like that. But he's too nice a guy to call anyone any names, so that doesn't mean anything. Being gay probably doesn't even enter into his consciousness.

"Oh, well. *Pagyvensim ir pažiūrėsim.*" LOL. That's Dad's phrase. "We'll live a while and we'll see." Whenever he's not sure about something, that's what he says. I never appreciated why he says it so often. Maybe now I do, at least a little bit. It means he's trying to figure things out in a complicated world. I guess even at his age he still has things to figure out in life, just like I do.

*

Carole and I were sharing a slice in Joe's Pizza.

"So, how's your sophomore year starting out?" she asked me.

I shrugged. "I don't know. Okay, I suppose. How's yours?"

She made a face. "I think I'm in sophomore slump. I can't concentrate."

"You mean on your classes?" I know what she really meant, and I couldn't help teasing her, telling her she had to find a way to take her mind off her French boyfriend.

She looked upset. "He's not my boyfriend. He's just a friend." But then she started giggling. "Well, maybe he is. I don't know. We never formalized anything." She got serious again. "See what I mean? I'm all over the place. How am I going to stand it until he comes here in December?"

I listened to her complain a little while longer. Then she finally turned her attention back to me. "So, what's going on with your love life?" she asked. "Met anybody yet?"

I shook my head. If only I could tell her about Bobby and what was going on between us—or more accurately, not going on. But I remembered how Bobby reacted when

I confessed to him that I had told Mr. Aniso about him and me. There was no way I was going to take a chance on that happening again by telling Carole.

Carole was looking at me intently. "You're blushing, RV."

"No."

"Oh, yes, you are. Beet red. C'mon, what are you hiding from me?" When I didn't answer she wheedled, "RV."

"Nothing."

"Okay, have it your way," she said. She settled back in the booth and shook her head. "You know, RV, one of these days you'll have to learn to be less secretive about the gay stuff. The sooner you do, the better it will be for you." I couldn't help feeling like a little kid being scolded by a parent or teacher.

We kept on eating our pizza, but Carole wouldn't let the subject drop.

"Have you said anything to your parents?" she asked.

"No."

"Why not?"

"Carole, stop interrogating me."

"I'm sorry. I don't mean to do that. I just want what's best for you. You know, in France people are much more blasé about sex."

I saw a chance to get Carole's attention off me and back to herself. "Oh? How do you know?"

A flirtatious, secretive look crossed her face. "I just know. From being with people."

"François?"

"François. And other people."

"Now who's blushing," I said, pointing my finger at her. "How many boyfriends did you have?"

"I told you. No boyfriends. There were just...some guys I made out with."

"Is that all you did?"

"Yeah." She paused and blushed more deeply. "Mostly. With a few other things."

"What other things?"

"Never mind."

"Woo-boy! No wonder I didn't hear from you for long stretches. You were busy with all those boyfriends all summer."

"RV, stop it." But she was smiling. "Yeah. It was a great summer." Then the smile turned into something sad. And now it's over," she added. "How are we going to get through the fall?"

"We'll have to manage," I said. "There are a lot of other things to worry about."

"Yeah. You're right." But I could tell Carole's mind was not on the fall but on the summer, back in Paris.

*

I'm sitting here thinking about my conversation with Carole. She does have a way of zeroing in on things that matter, even if I don't want to admit it. Why can't I be more open about myself, especially the gay stuff? Why am I trying to keep stuff from Mom and Dad? Why am I spending so much time feeling sorry for myself when it comes to Bobby?

Yeah, admit it, RV, you're feeling sorry for yourself. So, do something about it. Like what? I have no idea.

Jeez, look at me. Carole said her feelings were all over the place. What about me? I'm just as bad when it comes to Bobby. Maybe I'm in sophomore slump too.

Maybe I should talk to Mr. Aniso. Man, am I always going to keep running to him every time I have a problem? When am I going to stop? I'm fifteen years old and not a kid anymore. I should learn to solve my own relationship issues. I don't want to bother the guy so that he'll run in the other direction the minute he sees me. I bet there's only so much advice-giving even Mr. Aniso can manage before he gets sick of it.

Let me just turn off all these thoughts. I've got to relax and start on my homework. LOL. Most normal people hate doing homework, don't they? But I'm not normal. Not that I love homework, but most of the time, I know what I'm doing—except in Chemistry, of course. So, knowing what I'm doing in at least one aspect of my life gives me something good to think about. Let's see...

yo había amado

tu habías amado

el/ella había amado

nosotros habíamos amado

vosotros habíais amado

ellos/ellas habían amado

Yes! How's that, Señorita Sánchez? I'm not in sophomore slump, am I?

Chapter Three

Our End of the Bargain

Bobby stopped me in the corridor at school today. *Finally!* I thought. Bobby will apologize for being so busy and will ask if we want to get together.

But no such luck. After saying hi, he smiled that easygoing smile of his.

I smiled back. "Hi, Bobby."

"Are you still interested in seeing one of our football games?" Bobby asked. He didn't look at all upset or apologetic that we hadn't talked or spent any time together in over two weeks.

"Uh, yeah, sure."

"Great. We're playing Concord-Carlisle this weekend. That snooty school north of Boston. A big game for us. They beat our pants off too many times, but we should be ready this year. It should be a really exciting game."

"You're playing?"

"Yup. I'm first string."

"Oh, great," I said, trying to sound enthusiastic.

"Excellent. Knowing you're cheering for me will give me even more motivation." Then Bobby patted me on the shoulder. "Thanks, RV. OK. I gotta run." And he was off to his next class.

He did turn around and shout, "It will be a fantastic game! Go Wolfpack!" Then he turned around again and was off.

I tried not to let any disappointment show on my face. Yes, Bobby said my being there would motivate him, but he seemed much more excited about the game itself. As if I needed another reminder. He's one of the Wolfpack, the Latin team. That's the most important thing in the world to him. I'm second. If that.

I tried to reason myself out of my disappointment for the rest of the day. I told myself I wasn't being fair. I knew how important football was to Bobby. I was acting like a kid with a crush who can't think of anything else.

I forced myself out of my funk and called Carole to ask her to go to the game with me. But she was busy. "I'm seeing Tim and Loretta this Saturday," she told me.

Funny she should say that. I'd avoided asking her about Tim and the computer business, not wanting to get involved anymore. And I figured I would ask her for an update when the right time came.

This was the right time. "So, what's happening with the computer business?" I asked her.

"Oh, I'm letting Tim and Loretta do most of the work," she said. "I don't think I'll have much time for it this year." She turned to me and smiled a little. "I'm not totally out of it, don't worry. I'm still a consultant. And I still get a small share of the profits."

Good ol' Carole the businesswoman. I was happy for her, but not me.

"When were you going to tell me about it?" I couldn't help asking. "Do I get anything?"

She shook her head.

"No, sorry. I thought you were out of it already. From what Tim was telling me."

"Yeah. I guess whatever Tim says, goes. He's the take-charge type. Isn't he?" I bit my lip so I wouldn't say anything else.

But Carole caught the edge in my voice. She didn't say anything. And I didn't say anything either.

Great. An awkward silence between Carole and me. Not how I wanted this conversation to turn out.

"Okay, Carole. Good luck turning over the computer business," I finally said lamely.

"Thanks," she said. "Enjoy the game." And she ended the call. I got the feeling she couldn't wait to get off the line as quickly as she could.

*

"How much do you know about football?" Mark asked me.

"Pretty much nothing. You?"

"A little. I've gone to a few games with my parents and brother. One of our family outings."

I let out a laugh. "We never did that. Does that mean my family is un-American?"

Mark laughed too. "Maybe. If liking football is how you define being American."

With Carole busy, I asked Mark to come to Bobby's football game with me, and he agreed. That was a nice surprise. Mark and I are becoming more and more friendly at school, but this was the first occasion we'd spend time together outside school. I'm glad he said yes. Mark often looks a little sad, and I don't know if it's just the way his face is formed or if he really does feel sad so often. But he's a nice guy, and I still like being with him. It's better than being alone, especially when I'm going to my first football game.

"You've never been to a football game?" Mark asked, when we arrived at the game and I reminded him it was my first time. "I thought everyone has been to at least one football game."

"I told you, my parents are more into communists and fascists," I said, by way of explanation.

But that produced a strange, frightened look on Mark's face.

"No, no," l laughed again. "They're not communists or fascists." I told him more about our immigrant background. "They're more into capitalists now, though they complain about them, too, especially my Dad."

"Oh, okay." Mark nodded. He looked relieved. "Not that my family are such big football fans either. They're more into church stuff. That's what's important to my folks."

I nodded. "Yeah. Being Catholic is important for my folks, especially my mom." We were both silent for a minute, probably wondering about our own feelings toward religion.

Mark broke the silence. "Let's concentrate on the game."

"Yeah, okay," I agreed, turning my attention to what was happening on the field.

Bobby did great in the beginning. Toward the end of the first quarter, he caught one pass from the quarterback and ran a long way with the ball, going from left to right, managing to avoid everyone who tried to block his path.

Mark said it's called "juking," a way to evade tacklers.

I made a mental note to congratulate Bobby on his juking.

"Look at him go!" Mark yelled as Bobby kept running. "Juking and spinning his way from left to right, gaining yards."

"Go, Bobby, go!" I yelled along with the rest of the crowd.

But Bobby was tackled not too far from the end zone. No touchdown.

In the second quarter, Bobby caught one or two more passes but was tackled on both of those before he could get very far. Not that I understood everything that happened during the first half, but I knew enough to appreciate that Latin did pretty well. At halftime, the score was Concord-Carlisle 17, Boston Latin School 14.

I looked around the stands to see if I could spot Bobby's parents. I knew they'd be so proud of him, and I wanted to get a glimpse of their faces so I could tell Bobby about it later. But no such luck. Couldn't spot his parents in the multitude of faces, though I kept trying.

It was getting cold. Looking around the stands, I saw other people had brought thermoses and warm drinks with them. Just looking at the steam rising from their cups made me wish Mark and I had done the same thing.

"Hey, who is your favorite?" Mark asked, taking my mind off the temperature. He started pointing to different cheerleaders as they ran onto the field for a halftime cheering session.

I shrugged. "Not sure." I was impressed with all of them, as they started cheering and jumping and doing all sorts of complicated gymnastic movements.

"I like the blonde with the red ribbon in her hair," Mark said.

"Yeah. She moves pretty well."

"She's in my English class. Her name is Lavinia. Talk about great moves. Her body puts Miss Sánchez to shame."

"I didn't know any girl's body could put Miss Sánchez's to shame," I said, laughing as Mark poked me in the ribs. "This one comes close though."

Mark made a few more comments about the girl's looks to which I tried to agree. Not that I didn't think she was pretty, but she just didn't catch my attention. Not like that anyway.

There was the gay thing again. Could I tell Mark I was wrestling with my feelings about Bobby? I glanced over at him. He was engrossed in the moves of the cheerleaders. I looked away. No. Not now anyway. Maybe if we became better friends and told each other some secrets. Then maybe I could trust him.

I was glad when the second half started and I could turn my attention to the game again. Bobby didn't do anything particularly exciting, but I tried to cheer on the team anyway, shouting and clapping whenever Latin scored. Mark looked like he was having a good time, too, shouting and cheering even louder than me. But Latin was falling behind, bit by bit, no matter how loud our cheering got.

But then Bobby caught another pass and started running again toward the end zone. I was getting ready for the loudest cheer of my life, when suddenly he was tackled by a huge guy who came out of nowhere. One of the linemen, Mark explained, the biggest guys on the field. And then more guys from Concord-Carlisle piled onto the two of them.

Mark groaned. I groaned. A lot of people around us groaned.

Mark and I exchanged *oh, well. Better luck next time* looks and waited for Bobby to get up and the game to restart.

But Bobby didn't get up. A coach ran onto the field toward Bobby. And then a few more people. The guys around Bobby moved away, giving him some space.

Bobby was hurt. I swore under my breath, frustrated that I couldn't see what was going on. I stood up to get a better view, but it didn't help.

I heard a few murmurs in the crowd around us.

"I hope he's not hurt bad," Mark said.

"I hope not," I said, trying to sound calm, even though I wasn't feeling calm.

Finally, I saw Bobby get up, helped by one of the men.

"Thank God!" I said.

"Yeah," Mark agreed.

Bobby was talking to the men. I saw him shake his head. They talked some more. Then with the help of one of the men, Bobby limped slowly off the field.

"At least he wasn't carried off on a stretcher," Mark pointed out.

"Please, let's not even think about that," I said.

With Bobby out of the game, I had a hard time concentrating on it anymore. I don't know if it was my imagination, but the Latin team seemed to lose a bit of steam too. We cheered as best we could, but in the end the score was 31 to 24 in Concord-Carlisle's favor.

"I wish I could say good game," I told Mark as we were leaving. "At least it wasn't a blowout."

Mark nodded. "Yeah. Too bad your friend got injured. Hope he's okay."

"Yeah, me too. I'll call him tonight."

Mark put his hand on my shoulder. "So, not a great start for your first football game," he said sympathetically.

I nodded. "Yeah, I guess not."

"There will be better ones."

I appreciated his attempt at trying to make me feel better. "Thanks," I responded. "Of course, there will be."

*

"Hey, Bobby. How are you doing?"

"I'm okay," he answered.

I called him as soon as I got home. He didn't sound okay to me.

"I've been sleeping," he told me.

"Oh, I'm sorry," I said. "I just wanted to make sure you were all right. That tackle looked pretty bad. And then when you didn't get up..." I didn't want to remember what I was thinking at that moment.

"Thanks, RV," he said. "Yeah, I got a little banged up. I think I saw stars." He tried to laugh, but it sounded more like a croak.

"Stars?"

"Yeah. I didn't know people really saw stars when they got banged up. But I guess they do."

"Wow," was all I could manage to say.

"The coaches wanted me to go to the doctor to be checked out, but I told them I'm fine."

"You sure?"

"Yeah. Nothing's broken. I just got a little banged up, as I said." He tried to laugh again. "Thank God for these sturdy helmets. Now I know why we wear them."

There was an awkward pause, and I sensed that he wanted to get off the phone.

"Hey, RV. I need to catch up on my sleep," he said. "I'll be fine after some rest."

"Okay. I'll let you go. I just wanted to make sure you were all right."

"Thanks, RV. Oh, and RV," he added. "I appreciate your coming to the game. Sorry we couldn't give you a better outcome."

"There will be other games. Right?"

"Right."

And we finished the call.

*

I was still thinking about Bobby when I went down to dinner, but Mom and Dad's discussion soon got my full attention.

There's a rumor going around that the West Roxbury Catholic churches are going to merge, and one of them is going to be torn down for a new construction project. Mom is very upset, but Dad doesn't think it's so bad.

He told her the construction project was going to be big if it happened the way it was planned. And that meant jobs. A lot of jobs.

Mom thought that was all fine and dandy, but she didn't like the thought of one of the churches closing. There were already too few churches, in her opinion. And what about the schools associated with the churches? They were already too crowded, she said.

I've heard about the rumors, but now it suddenly seems personal. I hope it doesn't mean future arguments. Mom and Dad have been relatively okay since the summer. Nice to have some peace around the dinner table. Ray's still in a good mood, which is so weird. Good, but weird. Mom's happy with her part-time job and is working with her friend from work, Myrna, on her jewelry business. Dad still complains a little, mostly about his pay being cut last year, but he doesn't seem to be in danger of losing his job, at least not at the moment.

If Mom and Dad start arguing again, I know what'll happen. I'll start to get more pressure. Like today. It happened already.

"So, how are your classes, RV?"

"You like all your teachers, RV?"

"Keeping up with your homework, RV?"

"You're feeling good about that big test coming up, RV?"

And on and on, of course, in the Mother Tongue, since we don't speak English at home. I wish I hadn't told them about the PSAT test coming up. Sure, I'm a little nervous about it. Everyone's a little nervous about it. It's so hilarious. Everyone says they don't want to put too much pressure on us sophomores, that it's a little too early to get stressed out about college. But then at the same time they talk about the importance of tests and how the PSAT is good prep for the SATs next year. So, it's important to get into exam mode and do the best we can.

So, which is it? Worry or not worry, ha ha. You can't win.

And of course, Mom and Dad are after me to do well. What did Mom say to me one time? "We didn't come to this country so you kids could be mediocre." Or something like that in the Mother Tongue.

I guess I can't blame them totally. They've gone through a lot and work hard for their money. They want Ray and me to do well, but they can't afford the tuition of the best schools. Unless I get a big scholarship or a lot of financial aid, who knows where I'll end up. Many kids are in the same boat. So, we already feel that pressure big time, no matter what anyone says.

It pisses me off sometimes. The pressure to succeed is so important to Mom and Dad. It's always there. I can see it in their eyes. And I know what they're thinking. "We moved here for a better life. Not just for us. But for you kids. Especially for you kids." If Ray and I screw up, just a little bit, they get upset. That's the bargain, isn't it? We get a better life, but we better not screw up. We better be winners. Not mediocre.

Mom and Dad made that bargain with us, didn't they? Except we had no say in making it. It's just there, and I have to deal with it. What would happen if I became like Ray and didn't care about the bargain I had no say in making?

Chapter Four

Being Braver

Now I know why Ray is in such a good mood. He's got a new girlfriend. I heard them in the woods this afternoon.

Yeah, I was there after school. Sitting on my favorite rock and thinking about nothing and everything. It was such a great afternoon, one of those fall days where the sun is warm and shining brightly. And when the breeze blows, it makes the leaves with their multitude of colors look iridescent.

Wow, I'm being poetic again. Reminds me of how much Bobby likes it when I get poetic. I better stop thinking about it. Bobby used to like it. Who knows what he likes now? He's not around to hear me these days. His choice, not mine.

Anyway, I was sitting there on my rock. And who could I tell was not far away? Yeah, Ray. He was with a girl. But from her voice I could tell it wasn't the same girl he was with this summer. It was someone different. And there was no smell of pot or cigarettes. Ray and the girl were just talking softly. Sometimes I'd hear one of them giggle and then they'd talk softly again.

Their voices got closer. They were right near me behind some bushes. I froze. It was too late to get off the rock and leave. They'd hear me. But what if they moved or peeked through the bushes and saw me. They'd think I was spying on them.

There was a rustle of leaves as if they were sitting down on the ground, and then they grew quiet. I was sure they saw me. But then I heard them talking again in soft voices.

"I like you," the girl said.

"I like you too," Ray said.

They both giggled. Then Ray must have done something, because I heard the girl say, "That was nice."

"I like you a lot," Ray said.

"I like you a lot."

"Can I kiss you again?"

"Yeah."

I stayed frozen, almost afraid to breathe. I tried to think of what I'd say when they walked through the bushes and saw me.

"Oh, it's late. My mother will kill me," I heard the girl say. And sure enough, they got up, parted the bushes, and there they were staring me as they wiped some leaves off their clothes.

"Ray. Hi," I said.

"Hi," Ray said. He looked more embarrassed than angry.

I tried to make light of the situation even though I was even more embarrassed. "You guys discovered my favorite place."

Ray was silent. "I'm sorry," the girl said. "We didn't mean to." She looked more scared than embarrassed.

I kept trying to keep it light. "No biggie," I said. "We can all enjoy the view. Isn't it nice?" I gestured toward the hills in the distance.

The girl looked over in that direction and nodded, but she didn't say anything. She seemed nice, probably someone Ray met at school. She even had a small book bag by her side. I felt bad she looked so nervous.

"I'm Ray's brother, RV," I said.

"I'm Roberta," the girl said.

"Nice to meet you."

"Nice to meet you too."

More silence. Didn't Roberta say her mother was waiting for her? But she didn't make a move. She just glanced over at Ray, and then back to me.

Ray finally spoke up. "We gotta go," he said. "Roberta's late."

"Okay," I said. "Nice to meet you," I repeated.

"Nice to meet you too," Roberta said again.

"Bye."

"Bye."

Then Roberta picked up her book bag, and she and Ray disappeared down the path.

Ray played it cool at dinner and didn't say anything. But then afterward, when I was walking by his room to mine, he called out to me.

"Hey, RV. So, you met Roberta," he said, taking off his headphones when I walked into the room.

I sometimes wonder if he uses the headphones not only to listen to his music but even more to drown out the sounds of the rest of his family. Can't blame him, I guess.

"I'm sorry. I didn't mean to spy on you guys or anything," I said. "I was already sitting there when you guys came along."

"That's okay," Ray said. That was nice of him, but then he had to get in a little dig. "We weren't doing anything bad so there was nothing for you to see or report to Mom and Dad. Right? Right?" he repeated when I didn't answer right away.

I didn't want this to turn into another argument. "Roberta seems nice." I ignored Ray's little dig and tried to change the subject. And I really meant what I said about Roberta. For once, Ray seemed to be hanging out with a good person, not someone who could get him into trouble.

Ray nodded at my compliment. "Yeah, she is nice."

"You know her from school?"

"Yeah." Then he shrugged. "We'll just have to find another place to make out."

Was that meant to be another piece of information about him and Roberta? I didn't want to go there. Instead, I said with a little laugh, "Okay. I like my rock. I don't want to move."

"Is that where you go to make out?" Ray asked.

Boom! Where did that come from? Was Ray fishing for information about me? I didn't want to go there either. But I'm sure I was blushing, thinking about Carole and Bobby.

"Yeah," I nodded, trying to hide it.

"Okay. Maybe I'll catch you one of these days." Ray signaled the conversation was over by putting his headphones back on and getting back to his music.

I left his room, still wondering about Ray's question. Catching me with Carole wouldn't be a big deal, but that was over anyway. What would it be like if Ray caught me with Bobby? Maybe he'd be cool. He pretended to be cool about so many things. It would be nice to share something like that with my brother, wouldn't it? I still smile when I remember him telling Mom and Dad about bisexuals.

But as I went back to my room, any smiling disappeared as quickly as it started when I thought about Bobby. How would he react if we were caught kissing? Bobby was already paranoid about things.

I tried to forget about it. Concentrating on homework always helps block out other problems of life, doesn't it? Besides, the way things are going, who knows if Bobby and I will be sitting on that rock together ever again?

*

I had another crazy dream last night. Where do these dreams come from?

I was sitting with Mark watching Bobby's football game. But then Bobby came up to us, sat down next to Mark, and started watching the game too. Bobby and Mark started joking and talking like they were old friends. Bobby was smiling that great smile of his and having a good time. I tried to join in the conversation, but Bobby's attention was turned to Mark, not me. He was ignoring me totally. They left when Bobby promised to help Mark practice some football moves. He didn't even say goodbye to me. I jumped up, hoping to follow them, and then I woke up.

What an upsetting dream. Am I really that paranoid? I'm scared that Bobby might like someone else? Mark, of all people? At least Bobby was happy in the dream, smiling his big smile. I tried to keep that image in my mind, even though it made me sad that Bobby wasn't smiling at me.

There I was, lying in bed, trying to hold onto that image of Bobby's smiling face. This is stupid, I told myself, but I pretended it was me Bobby was smiling at, not Mark. And what did I do? Yeah, gotta admit this. I jerked off. The Big M.

Not that it's the first time I've done the Big M in the middle of the night. Not by a long shot. But last night it was more intense. Like holding onto Bobby and his smile was the most important thing in the world.

The Big M still drives me crazy. But I can't stop doing it. So many thoughts flying around in my head about it. When I was in grammar school, I could tell the priests and nuns didn't like us doing it. They didn't even like talking about it, except that one lesson we had with Father What's-His-Name. Father What's-His-Name said it wasn't ideal, because Catholics believe the ideal is to get married and have kids. But he didn't have a good answer when we asked him if something that wasn't ideal could still be pretty nice. Maybe a B, instead of an A, just like Mark and I are called in Latin School, ha ha.

And then there was the time Bobby wanted to do the Big M with me and I got scared. That still bothers me. A lot. Bobby called me innocent. So, if I don't want to be innocent, do I have to try to do it with someone? Who? Mark? He seems like the innocent type like me, which is why I like him. So that probably wouldn't fly. Though you never know, right?

As I was lying there, thinking about Mark, I could tell I was blushing. Even in the dark. In the middle of the night. Crazy. Why does thinking about doing the Big M with Mark make me blush? As if it's wrong. Is it something that should only be done alone?

Maybe that's the trouble. I already do too many things alone. Mark and I are getting to be better friends and have started doing some things together, but there's no one else. Carole's off in la-la land, thinking about François. And Bobby. Who knows? I guess there's Mr. Aniso. I know I could go to him if I had a real problem. But like I've said, I can't run to him for every single little thing.

"Hey, Mr. Aniso. Did you do the Big M when you were in high school? Or the seminary? Did it screw you up in any way?"

Ha ha. Wonder what he'd say. Too bad I can't ask him. Just one of those things people don't talk about.

So, there's only God. And who knows what I think of Him these days. "Hey, Big Guy. What do you think of the Big M? Why don't people talk about it? Do people in heaven do it? Why did you invent it?"

I wish I were sure God existed in the first place. But there I go with all my questions again. Life has too many questions. Or maybe it's just me. If I didn't ask so many questions, what would life be like?

*

Mr. Aniso stopped me in the corridor today.

"Hey, RV," he said. "How are you?"

"Fine," I answered, my usual response when I don't quite know what to say.

"I'm sorry you're not in my Latin class this year. I feel like I haven't seen you in ages."

I didn't quite know what to say so I stayed quiet.

"I miss our talks," he added.

"I do too," I finally responded, the words just popping out of my mouth. "I don't want to bother you too much because, well, I know everyone's busy."

"You should never feel that I'm too busy to talk to you." Mr. Aniso gave me that serious look that reminded me of how Mom and Dad look at me sometimes. "Is everything okay? You're enjoying sophomore year?"

I nodded. "Yeah, sure." Then I couldn't help adding, "Like always, there are some classes that are better than others."

Mr. Aniso let out a laugh. "I bet. I remember how much I hated chemistry in high school."

That made me laugh as well. "Really? That's the subject I hate the most too!" We both laughed and made some jokes about chemistry. What is it about Mr. Aniso that makes me feel so comfortable with him? Standing there I realized how much I did miss him. "Are you sure it's okay to call you if...if I ever have a question about anything," I blurted out.

"Of course, it is!" Mr. Aniso said. "I hope you know that by now."

I nodded. "Yeah, sure. But you know how it is. I don't want to bother you with every little thing and—"

"RV. I'll say it just once more," Mr. Aniso interrupted me. "Don't ever think you're bothering me!

Okay?" He suddenly looked serious again. So serious I thought he was going to grab me by my shoulder the way he always does when he wants to tell me something important.

But he didn't. He just kept looking at me with that serious expression until I said, "Okay, thanks, Mr. Aniso. I promise I'll never think I'm bothering you."

"You sure?"

I nodded. "Yes."

"Okay." Mr. Aniso was smiling again. Then he pointed a finger at me. "Remember, I'll hold you to that promise."

"I'll keep it. I'll keep it," I answered. Then we both laughed again before we said goodbye and parted.

*

I was feeling better walking to my next class after seeing Mr. Aniso. Not that I have anything in particular to ask him at the moment—except all my zillions of questions, of course, that are popping up in my head all the time. But I know despite what he said, that's not what Mr. Aniso was talking about. He made me promise to talk to him if I ever feel down or something serious is bothering me. Not asking him about the Big Guy or why the world works a certain way. Not even Mr. Aniso can help me with those questions. Those I have to learn by myself. Like why this year's Latin teacher, Miss Wagstaff, screeches the way she does. Latin was my next class, and I tried not to think how much better it would be if Mr. Aniso taught it. Even when Miss Wagstaff called on me, asked me to stand up and conjugate "to love." Since Lithuanian has conjugations, I get the concept.

Amo. I love.

Amas. You love, singular.

Amat. He or she loves.

Amamus. We love.

Amatis. You love, plural.

Amant. They love.

Ha! Take that, Miss Wagstaff, I said to myself, sitting back down in my seat. Since Lithuanian works the same way, conjugations are a piece of cake. There are some benefits to being a kid of immigrants, ha.

I shouldn't have been so proud of myself. As I sat down and Miss Wagstaff started calling other kids, I saw Duffy look over at me and smirk. (Great word, smirk. It's a laugh, but not a friendly one. What you expect from gangsters.) Duffy's going to be a gangster, I'm sure. He and his pal Doyle are probably the ones who beat up Mr. Aniso last year, though no one can prove it. Or they hired someone to do it gangster-style. How they're still in Latin School, I have no idea. Except they're smart, which makes them even scarier. At least I notice this year they're usually in separate classes. Probably intentional. But that doesn't mean they can't get together after class. And I don't want to be on the other side of that smirk. I still remember how they threw that kid McGrath against the lockers. He dribbled down to the floor like overdone lasagna.

I put Duffy out of my mind and tried to stay inconspicuous as Miss Wagstaff called on other kids. (Inconspicuous, another great word in my repertoire. The next best thing to being invisible.). Anyway, I was trying to act inconspicuous when Miss Wagstaff called on me again.

"RV. Did you read yesterday's assignment on the ablative absolute?"

"Oh, ah, no."

"You didn't? Did-*n't*?" she repeated. There was that voice, on its way to screeching.

"I-I'm sorry. I was busy with a Spanish assignment. I-I was going to do it tonight."

"To-*night*? It was supposed to be done *last night*!"

I stood there like a fool. Not like me to flub off homework.

Miss Wagstaff screeched a little bit more and made me sit down. She then turned to the other kids.

A smarty-pants guy named Censulla raised his hand. "The ablative absolute acts as an adverb. It modifies the predicate of the sentence," he said, sounding like the know-it-all he pretends to be. Then he gave some examples in Latin.

"Very *good*!" Miss Wagstaff said.

I gotta hand it to Censulla. He might be a smarty-pants, but he's out, way out. He makes no bones about being gay, and wears these flashy, jingly clothes to class that make him look even more gay.

I glanced over at Duffy and saw him look at Censulla with the same smirk he had on his face when he looked at me. Maybe even more gangster-like. I said a little prayer, thanking someone up there. Maybe it was good that I didn't have time to do the assignment. I'd rather have a disapproving screech from Miss Wagstaff than a smirk from Duffy. The last thing I need is to be teacher's pet in this class, the way I was with Mr. Aniso. That would surely get me on Duffy's bad side. And probably thrown against the lockers. Glad there's someone else in this class who'll looks like he'll be the teacher's pet.

Still, to be safe, I tried to be inconspicuous at the end of class, grabbing my books and leaving as quickly as I could. Duffy was leaving with a few of his friends too. As they passed me talking and laughing, I thought I heard Duffy mumble "faggot." Was it directed at me? Or Censulla, who was walking nearby? Or both of us? I was afraid to look at them and quickly walked away.

It made me feel bad the rest of the day. I don't particularly want anything to do with Censulla. I feel like he's in a totally different world from me. But I gotta admit, I admire how out there he is and brave about himself. Not like me, who's afraid of his own shadow some days.

RV. You gotta promise yourself to be braver. Right now! But how? I'm not like Censulla. Then who am I like? I still have so many questions about everything, including myself, I wouldn't know how to be braver even if I wanted to be.

Chapter Five

Faggots: Real or Imagined

We returned to the old days at dinner. I knew peace wouldn't last that long. Not that it was terrible, but my stomach was churning through most of the meal, since it seemed like it could get worse any moment.

It's Saturday. Mom was out protesting earlier today. Yeah, Mom. The merging of the churches and planning for the construction project are moving along, at least if you believe the news. A big protest was planned in front of one of the churches, Holy Name, whose grammar school I went to. Mom was there, holding up a placard and demanding a full hearing in front of the public before anything was done. The protesters were joined by nuns and priests not only from Holy Name but from St. Theresa's, the church that might merge with Holy Name. Nuns and priests from other churches in Boston were at the demonstration too.

The protest came up at dinner. Dad said that priests and nuns should be tending to the sick and poor, not protesting. Mom disagreed. Asked him if he was happy that churches were closing.

He responded no but that it was a sign of the times.

Mom responded back that when times were not good people should not sit by and let things happen without doing something about it.

Dad asked her what she thought about all the jobs that would be created by construction of the new development. People would be helped in a different way.

Mom answered that it was not always about money. New jobs could be created in other ways.

Any mention of money always gets Dad riled up. He asked her how she would feel if he lost his job and they had no money. So, he's worrying about his job again. I guess that's never far from his mind, especially since his pay was cut last year.

They kept going back and forth. Dad said now that Mom's a citizen she feels empowered to protest. Mom said, yes, certainly, that's what citizenship is about. She added that a lawsuit has been filed by the protest group she belongs to. So, she was hoping the merger and the planned development could be stopped.

In the middle of their discussion, Ray took out his cell phone and put in an earbud so he could listen to music. Dad told him to put away his phone, as he usually does. But he really wasn't paying much attention to Ray. He quickly turned back to Mom to say something else about the protest and the lawsuit.

But Mom noticed. She asked Ray where he got the earbuds since they hadn't bought a pair for him. He told her he got them from a friend.

"What friend?" Both Mom and Dad wanted to know.

"*Jūs manim netikit?*" "You don't trust me?" Ray is so good at deflecting blame from himself.

Mom and Dad were forced to forget their discussion for a minute and focus on Ray. They defended themselves and said they trusted him. They told him they were just wondering who would give him earbuds since they were expensive. Can't blame them. I'm sure they were thinking about the time Dad was called by the school principal to come in with Ray to discuss some missing equipment.

Ray told them the earbuds were not expensive and that his friend Roberta had given them to him because she got better ones for a birthday present.

Mom and Dad exchanged glances, looking like they didn't know what to say. Then they started asking Ray about Roberta, but Ray just shrugged, saying she was a friend from school. Then he told them to ask me, since I had met her.

So, they turned to me. I told them I did meet her and that she seemed like a nice person. Didn't say where though. It's okay to keep some secrets, no? The last thing I wanted was to say something that would cause more questions.

That seemed to calm Mom and Dad down a bit, though neither one seemed too happy about it. Happily, the discussion about the protest seemed to have petered out. Dad ate the rest of his dinner grumbling to himself quietly, while Mom made a point of ignoring his grumbling and trying to act super cheerful.

"So, how's Roberta?" I asked, as I was passing by Ray's room after dinner. I guess I'm still trying to get him to open up to me a little bit. Am I trying to be a good older brother? Or a fool?

Lying on his bed, about to put his new earbuds in, Ray shrugged. "She's okay."

"You seeing each other this weekend?"

Ray shrugged again. "I'm not sure. Maybe."

Then he put in his earbuds and turned to his cell phone, signaling that the conversation was over.

Well, at least he didn't tell me it was none of my business. I should count that as a victory, right? So sad what counts as a victory in our family.

I laughed when I flopped down on my own bed. Laughed at myself. I was so preoccupied with Ray and Roberta and Mom and Dad, what about me? What were my plans for the rest of the weekend? None. Bobby hasn't called, of course, probably busy with practice and another game Saturday. What about Sunday? Carole has been out shopping with her mother, which she seems to be doing a lot of these days. I thought about calling Mark, but then stopped, remembering Mark had said he'd be busy all weekend, attending some Christian Fellowship meeting with his parents.

So, it's me, myself, and I for most of the weekend. Well, at least it will be quiet. I don't argue with myself. Not much anyway.

*

"RV, háblame sobre la geografía de España."

"¿La geografía?"

"Si, la capital, las ciudades mas grandes, las regiones."

"La capital es Madrid. Otras ciudades pequeñas son Barcelona y Sevilla."

"RV. No, no. No pequeñas. Grandes. Las ciudades mas grandes."

"Oh. Otras ciudades grandes son Barcelona y Sevilla."

"Muy bien, RV. Muy bien."

Phew. Miss Sánchez called on me practically the minute I walked into class. Dumb of me to mix up the words for smallest and biggest. But at least Miss Sánchez gave me a "very good" thumbs sign when I finished my example. Along with a nice smile.

Mark nudged me as I was sitting back down in my seat. "Nice smile," he whispered.

I nodded slightly, trying to ignore him, because I knew he'd want to make me laugh. But he nudged me again and whispered, "Lucky you. Why don't sexy women smile at me?"

I ignored Mark, but I couldn't help watching Miss Sánchez as she called on other people. Mark was right. She was sexy, very sexy. The tight gray sweater she was wearing accentuated her breasts.

I thought about Carole, the only girl I've kissed before. Her breasts were anthills compared to Miss Sánchez's. I couldn't help myself. Instead of paying attention for much of the class, I started fantasizing about what it would be like to make out with Miss Sánchez.

Mark teased me about Miss Sánchez when the class ended and we were leaving.

"C'mon. Don't you find her sexy?" he said.

"Yeah. So?" I said, trying to stay cool but feeling myself blush a little.

"I saw you looking at her breasts when she called on you."

"I was not."

"Yes, you were. Is that why you made the mistake in your answer? You were distracted."

"No."

"Yes. And then she gave you that big, beautiful smile. I'm jealous."

I was about to tease Mark back, when I heard someone say, "Out of the way!"

"What?" Mark said, starting to turn around.

"I said out of the way, faggot!" It was Duffy, who was walking behind us and tried to get by. When Mark didn't move out of the way fast enough, Duffy roughly nudged him aside and walked by us quickly.

Mark looked shaken.

"He and his friend Doyle are bad news," I said, not knowing how else to help Mark feel better.

"I know," he answered. "I guess he was just getting back at me."

"For what?"

"I did the same thing to him earlier this morning."

"You?" I couldn't imagine Mark being rude to anybody.

"I was late for English class, and Duffy and Doyle were in front of me. I didn't even notice it was them. I had my head down and was thinking about something else. Anyway, I sort of pushed between them and ran ahead, so I wouldn't be late for class." Mark looked up at me. "I said 'excuse me,' but I guess I must have nudged them a little."

"I told you, they're bad news. Just forget it."

"Yeah," Mark said. But he didn't look very convinced.

Later at lunch, I could see that Mark was still not himself.

"What's the matter?" I asked him. "You seem distracted."

"I do?"

I tried to tease him to lighten his mood. "You do. And you don't even have Miss Sánchez's breasts to distract you."

"Ha ha," he said. He smiled for a second, but then started frowning again.

"Mark, what's the matter?" I asked him a second time.

After a few moments of silence, he opened up a little. "Yeah, sorry. I'm just thinking about Duffy."

"Because of what happened this morning?"

"Yes. But more than that. I think he has it in for me."

"What makes you say that?"

"Just the way he looks at me sometimes. With a sneer."

"Sneer. That's better than smirk."

"What?"

I told Mark about the words I often think about. And how I used to think the look Duffy gave people was a smirk. "But sneer is much better," I said. "More evil."

I was trying to get Mark to forget Duffy, but I noticed that made him frown even more. "Mark, he looks at everybody like that. With that stupid sneer."

That didn't help. "What about him calling me faggot?" Mark asked.

"What about it?"

"Maybe he thinks I'm gay."

"So?"

"So? That's pretty bad."

"What if you were gay?"

"RV. Don't go there," Mark said.

"Okay," I said, not wanting to make him more upset, though that comment made me wonder what he was thinking. He stayed silent, brooding about something.

"Maybe you're right," he finally said after a while. "Maybe I am just being paranoid. "Let's just think about Miss Sánchez instead."

"Okay," I repeated. I tried to picture Miss Sánchez in her gray sweater, but that image was crowded out by the memory of Duffy when he gave me that look in Latin class. A smirk, a sneer, or whatever it was.

I left Mark to go to my next class, still wondering about what he had said. Did he mean it would be bad if he was gay or bad because it meant Duffy was after him? And what about me? Does Duffy think anyone who is nice and quiet can be picked on? Because they won't fight back? He's right about that. I'm no good at throwing punches. Not that I've ever tried, but I never want to. It's just not me. Is that why I'm a "faggot" in Duffy's eyes? What about

Mark? He doesn't seem like the type to ever throw a punch either. So, he's a "faggot" too?

Are we both "faggots"? What does Mark think about that? Should I confront him? Does that make him want to spend more time with me? Or back away?

Maybe I shouldn't. He's afraid to have anything to do with a faggot, real or imagined, isn't he? I should first ask myself if I want to spend time with him.

Chapter Six

Climate Change

October is zooming by. I've been trying to stay out of Duffy and Doyle's way. Trying to stay out of everyone's way, as a matter of fact. Focusing on schoolwork. Tried to prepare for the PSATs but there's only so much studying you can do for these tests, isn't there? I hope I did okay. At least in English. Though the math part didn't seem that difficult. Well, we'll see in December when we get our scores.

College entrance stress, here we come! Ha ha. I thought I promised myself not to think about all that yet. But I can't help it. Even though college acceptance is two years away, it seems to be on everyone's mind. Especially Mom and Dad's. "Study hard so you can get financial aid, RV." "We'll need your help, RV." "You'll go to the best college we can afford, RV." "Let's hope we keep our jobs, RV." Man, and they say sophomore year is supposed to be fun. Maybe for some people it is. But not for us worrywuss types who take everything seriously.

I went into Boston the other day. Went to see a movie about teenage guys in a small town in the Midwest, dealing with high school and sex and crazy parents. Hello! Sounded like my life, except nothing about being gay. Tried to get Carole and Mark to go, but they were both busy, so I went by myself. The movie was okay, even funny at times. It was R-rated because of a scene about one of the guys trying to seduce a sexy older woman in his neighborhood. Reminded me of Miss Sánchez. The guy tried hard, but he didn't know what he was doing. The Miss Sánchez character took off all her clothes, trying to help him along, but then they fell off the bed. Probably something I would do. At least I had no trouble getting into the movie, even though I'm not sixteen yet. So, I took pointers. If I see enough of these movies, maybe I can learn what not to do so I don't fall out of bed whomever I'm with.

Leaving the movie theatre, I walked by a crowd of people demonstrating about something. Looking at placards, I saw the word "gay" written on some of them. It turned out the people were demonstrating about a high school teacher who had been fired in a town near Boston. The teacher was gay and had assigned some gay-themed books to the students. Some parents were upset because the books were explicit about sex and the teacher had made some comments that the parents found offensive. This was a religious school, and the parents were upset because they said the comments went against their religious teachings. The school listened to these parents and fired the teacher.

This issue has become a big deal, and I've seen it on the news. I saw a few TV cameras there this time too. This was a demonstration in support of the teacher. They were trying to help him get his job back. There was another group of people across the street who agreed with the firing and were demonstrating to keep the teacher out of their school.

The two groups were shouting at each other back and forth. They were so loud it took me a while to hear that someone was calling my name. I turned around, and there was Mr. Aniso and his friend Ben coming up to me.

"Hey, RV!"

"Good to see you, RV."

I greeted both of them. They asked me what I was doing in town, and I told them I was heading home after the movie. They told me they've been demonstrating about this case for the past few weeks.

I asked them if they knew this teacher.

They said no, but that it was important to support someone who they thought was being treated unfairly.

"Let me ask you, RV," Ben said. "Do you think this is offensive?" He told me that the teacher had said he thought the religious teachings advocated by the school about sex and sexuality were misguided and out of date. "He was just trying to expose the students to another point of view. Is that so offensive?" he repeated.

I shook my head, though I hadn't really thought much about it before.

"Religion can be misguided, just like the rest of us," Mr. Aniso added.

We chatted for a few more minutes about how things were going, and then Mr. Aniso and Ben said they had to be going back to the demonstration. I said goodbye and went to get my train home.

I was thinking about the demonstration on the train. Mr. Aniso and Ben are certainly out, and it's good that they're demonstrating, right? What about me? I'd like to think I'd demonstrate if I thought someone was being treated unfairly. What about being gay? When will I be more sure about that? Will I ever be like Mr. Aniso and Ben? They seem so confident in themselves. Or even someone like Censulla, the know-it-all in Latin class. He's my age, but he seems as confident as Mr. Aniso and Ben. What does it take to get like that?

When I got home, the Big Guy reminded me He's still around, even though I haven't made up my mind about Him. But He likes those little curveballs He zings my way, doesn't He? Dinner tonight went off without an argument, which is always something to be thankful for. We only say grace during special occasions like holidays, but I should work that into my prayer the next time it's my turn to say it. "Thank you, Big Guy, for what we are about to receive. Please keep us from all arguments, snide comments, threats, broken dishes, and cell phone throwings. Amen."

Anyway, after dinner we all ended up together in the living room to watch TV. The news came on and what do

I see but the demonstration about the gay teacher who was fired.

And what else do I see? A shot of some people, including Mr. Aniso and Ben, shouting, "Ho, ho, hey, hey. Mr. Briggs has got to stay! Ho, ho, hey, hey. Mr. Briggs has got to stay!"

My heart skipped a few beats. Was this shot before or after I talked to them? Did I make it onto the news too?

I asked the Big Guy to stop my heart palpitations so I could better think and come up with what I'd say to Mom and Dad if I showed up on the TV screen. They were certainly paying attention to the arguments discussed on the newscast. Dad said since it was a religious school, they had a right to hire people who agreed with their philosophy. Even Mom didn't disagree. Since she's religious, she usually supports the church and other religious institutions, anyway.

Ray put his two cents in too. To him, of course, the issue was a no-brainer. He said people are too uptight about sex and everyone should do what they wanted.

Mom and Dad both turned to Ray. *Phew!* I thought, glad Mom and Dad's attention turned away from the TV and onto Ray.

They asked Ray what he knows about sex.

Ray told them plenty.

They asked how.

Ray said that everyone at school talks about sex a lot.

Looking concerned, Mom asked what he meant by a lot.

Ray backed down a little bit. He said not a lot but enough. And sex was natural, adding that people who were uptight about sex were morons.

That got Dad mad, asking Ray if he thought Mom and Dad were morons.

And so it went, back and forth. The good thing was when they turned back to the TV, the segment about the demonstration was off the air and we could drop the discussion about sex.

I watched the rest of the newscast and then was happy to leave and go up to my room.

Thanks again, Big Guy. You enjoy those little curveballs you throw at me, don't you? What would I have said if they did show me on TV with the demonstrators? Would I have made an excuse, or would I have said it was good that people were doing something they believed was right?

Listen to me. Sounding so confident about other people doing the right thing. But what about me, myself, and I? When will I be confident about RV Aleksandravičius? Mr. Aniso said that's where it all starts, doesn't it? With yourself.

*

I must have still been thinking about the demonstration as I was falling asleep, because I had another one of my crazy dreams. Ray, Dad, and I were preparing to go to a demonstration. But it was for Lithuania, nothing to do with gay rights. Even though Lithuania is now free, Dad still worries about it and all the relatives he has there. He thinks it will be taken over by the Russians any day. Of course, he's been saying that ever since I can remember.

But in the dream, Ray and I went along with him, taking our placards and planning to march with him in downtown Boston. Ray even asked that on our way we pick up his friend Roberta, who was going to march with us. But it took us longer to get to Roberta's house than we thought, so by the time we got to the demonstration, the people had marched off. Dad was frustrated. Then he saw another demonstration coming instead, the one for the gay teacher. It was headed by Mr. Aniso and Ben. When he saw that, Dad turned to me and asked angrily, "Are you with them or us?" Before I could answer, he drove us to City Hall and had us march in front of the entrance while chanting, "Hey, hey, ho, ho! The Russian imperialists have got to go!" "Hey, hey, ho, ho! The Russian imperialists have got to go!"

There we were, the four of us walking round and round in a circle like fools, holding our placards and stupidly chanting while a small group of people gathered to watch us. Some of the people watching us began to ask why weren't demonstrating for the gay teacher instead. Another person said, "Lithuania's free! You guys are behind the times!" I didn't know what to say, feeling embarrassed. Ray and Roberta looked ready to run away. Finally, I woke up.

Where do these dreams come from? I know about Sigmund Freud's theories. He was big into dreams. Maybe I should read one of his books. It might help me figure myself out. I don't expect any miracles but any clues to what my crazy unconscious comes up with at night might give me some clues about my conscious brain during the day.

*

"I'd like to invite you to a Halloween party."

"You're having a Halloween party?"

"No, Tim is. It's at his house. We're throwing it together."

I didn't know what to think. I wanted to see Carole, but Tim was another story. Then again, when was the last time I was invited to any party?

"Oh, come on," Carole said, when I hesitated. "It's for a good cause."

"A cause?"

"Yeah. Climate change. Tim is getting into that these days. We all have to think of ways to help our planet. Don't you agree?"

"Sure."

"So, you'll come, yes?"

"Yeah, sure." Trying to sound more excited, I said, "That sounds great."

Carole gave me the details. "Oh, one more thing," she added, giggling. "How could I forget?"

"What?"

"You have to wear a costume. No ifs, ands, or buts."

"I figured, since it's Halloween."

"The costume has to be on climate change."

"What?"

"Yeah."

"How am I supposed to dress like climate change?"

Carole giggled again. "Use your imagination, RV. At first Tim and I thought it was a little crazy, too, but the more we thought about it, the more examples we came up with."

"Like what?"

"Oh, okay. You can come as a tree. As an extinct species. As a thermometer."

"A thermometer?"

"You can't use any of these. Come up with something unique."

"Carole, I don't know—"

"Oh, RV. You'll come up with something. Think of it as a way making all of us aware how climate change applies to everyone. There will be prizes. It will be so much fun. Tim even invited a few of his teachers. When was the last time we had a big party like this?"

Never, I thought as I turned off my phone. I did want to go to the party. It would be great to spend time with Carole. I missed her giggling. I smiled, wondering what crazy costume she would come up with. Even when I thought of Tim, I kept on smiling. Maybe he wouldn't be so bad in a crowd of people. He certainly couldn't boss anyone around at a party. And what kind of costume would he come up with?

Okay, RV. Come up with a good costume, so that Tim can't lord it over you. Maybe I can get my crazy unconscious to help. It gives me crazy dreams. Why can't it give me some ideas of how to cope with real life?

*

I was standing in a corner with a cup of punch in my hand. I did make it to the party. I didn't see Carole or Tim when I got there, or anyone else I knew, so I put myself in the corner, my usual modus operandi at parties. (Good title for my autobiography? *RV's Modus Operandi of Life: What Not to Do, How Not to Live.*)

Finally, I saw Carole coming up to me. "Wow! Cool costume," she exclaimed. "What does it say?"

She started reading the words on the big piece of cardboard I was wearing. "The Carbon-Ator?"

"Yeah, thanks," I said, blushing a little, happily for a change. "This is an app. The Carbon-Ator app. I measure carbon footprint. You see all these buttons?" I asked, pointing to all the colored squares I had painted on the cardboard. "They measure the carbon footprint of the different activities I do during the day. Biking. Driving a car. Taking a plane. A train."

"I love it!" Carole jumped up and down and clapped her hands. "l knew you would come up with something good, RV!"

I started feeling better. Leave it to good ol' Carole to get me out of worrying about myself and doing something fun.

"Your costume is pretty neat too," I said. She was wearing a long, white sheet, which had neon pinwheels on short sticks attached to it. *Go Wind Power!* it said in Day-Glo colors on the front. And whenever she moved or twirled around, the shiny pinwheels turned too.

I gave her a hug, careful not to damage all those pinwheels. A few other people came by and complimented Carole on her costume. She twirled around again, obviously enjoying herself.

Then Tim came by. He was wearing a black sheet with a hood that hid his face. He was also carrying a scary-looking weapon like a machete or one of those reapers they cut wheat down with. He certainly looked like the Grim Reaper. When he got closer, I saw the words that were written all over the sheet: *Coal = Death. Fossil fuels = Death. Carbon = Death.*

Leave it to Tim to look scary. But I had to congratulate him. "Neat costume," I said.

"Thanks, yours too," he answered.

Tim turned to Carole. "Come," he said. "There's someone I want you to meet."

Carole give me a quick peck on the cheek and then twirled away with Tim.

To entertain myself, I stood in the corner watching everyone. People had really thought a lot about their costumes. One girl was walking around covered in what looked like dirty-gray gauze. "I'm greenhouse gases," I heard her tell someone. Another guy must have rented a polar bear costume. Except the fur was dripping wet and he kept wiping sweat off his brow. When he wiped what I guess was perspiration from his armpits, I moved as far away from him as I could. Another guy was wearing a map of Antarctica with a big X through it. Loretta, Tim's computer partner, was walking around with pictures of dead fish plastered on her dress. My favorite was a girl dressed in bright green with leafy cardboard trees growing out of her shoulders and from the top of her head. She was carrying a little basket filled with balloons that were blown up to the size of baseballs. "I'm the Amazon rain forest," she announced, as she walked around and gave out the balloons. "Oxygen here! Oxygen here, to save the planet!"

I was getting a little restless. Entertaining yourself only goes so far, doesn't it, even though I'm an expert at it.

Happily, just at that moment, someone tapped me on the shoulder.

"Hey, RV. Nice costume."

I turned around. It was Mark.

"Hey, Mark! I didn't know you were friends with Tim."

Mark shrugged and gave a sheepish smile. "I didn't either. But I got an invite. So here I am. Nice to see a friendly face."

"Yeah."

Mark was wearing a T-shirt with pictures of world leaders imprinted all over it. Except they all had their eyes closed, some with their heads tilted in one direction or the other. On his chest were the words "Actions Speak..." On his back were more pictures of sleeping presidents and prime ministers with the words "...Louder Than Words."

"I like your costume too," I said.

"Thanks."

We both stood there in the corner for a while. I pointed out other crazy costumes to Mark. He seemed a little down for some reason and didn't pay much attention to the people I was pointing out. I figured it was just Mark, looking sad again. I certainly know what that feels like.

To distract both of us, I suggested we go get some punch and snacks. We did and then went back to our corner. I told myself to go say hello to some other people. But I'm never good at coming up to strangers and introducing myself. So, I stayed in the corner, trying to talk to Mark.

Then I saw Carole. She was with Tim, talking to some teachers who had come by. Miss Sánchez wasn't there, but I saw Mr. Felucci, my math teacher, and some teachers I didn't recognize. They were listening to Tim who was talking about climate change. I didn't hear everything, but I overheard enough to see how confident Tim sounded. Another confident person. Where did he pick up all those facts and figures? I have to hand it to him. He knows a lot about computers. He knows a lot about climate change. What else does he know about? No wonder Carole is so smitten with him.

I was happy to turn my attention away from Tim when the front door opened, and more people came into the party. I recognized some members of the football team. I couldn't help it, feeling myself flush with excitement. Was Bobby coming too?

Nope. No Bobby. A sign of how things were going this Fall. I was starting to get used to not seeing Bobby, except for a minute or two in the school halls. Not a good sign.

I turned back to Mark, who was glancing around the room. "I wonder if Miss Sánchez is here," he said.

"I haven't seen her," I said. "I bet she'd think of a great costume."

"Yeah." Mark nodded, blushing a little bit.

I had to tease Mark, who obviously had a huge crush on Miss Sánchez. "I bet her costume would be pretty sexy. Don't you think?"

Mark blushed even redder. I guess that's why I like him more and more. He's another blusher, just like Carole and me. Any thoughts I had about not spending time with him have disappeared. Yeah, I suspect he has some weird thoughts about being gay. Or gay people. Or both. Maybe someday I'll find out what they are. For now, I can't think about that. He's too nice a guy to cut out as a friend. At least until I find out more.

I was about to tease Mark more about Miss Sánchez when Mr. Felucci cleared his throat and raised his hand, asking for quiet.

"First of all, let's thank Tim and his parents for making their house available for this great party," he said. Everyone applauded.

I couldn't believe it. The frown Mr. Felucci always has in class disappeared and he smiled. "I have an announcement," he continued when the applause died down. He motioned to the other teachers. "We've been talking, and we're really impressed with all the great costumes and energy we see here tonight. So, we teachers are forming a new committee to help you guys with any climate change initiatives you come up with. Whether it's demonstrating, coming up with new ideas, starting projects, raising money, getting the word out to the community, we'll be there to help you in whatever way we can."

"Yay! Yay!" Everyone applauded and cheered, including Mark and me. We started throwing around ideas, wondering how we could get involved too.

The party lasted for a few more hours. People danced and the music got louder. I was hoping to take

Carole out for a dance, but every time I made my way toward her, she was already dancing with either Tim or someone else. Then we voted for the Best Costume. The Amazon rain forest won. The sweaty polar bear guy got second place. I got an honorable mention.

At least I got to hug Carole when I was leaving. I couldn't believe I had hesitated about coming to the party. Tonight was one of those nights I felt I really belonged. Not just as a nerd studying hard to keep up with the other nerds in school, but as someone enjoying myself and doing something fun in life. Regular life! What a new feeling! Do other people feel this way a lot? Who knows? Who cares? I'm just trying to make tonight last as long as I can.

Chapter Seven

Stressful Lunches

"Hey, RV! Long time no see."

"Hey, Bobby!"

"Can I sit down?"

"Sure."

This was the school lunchroom, not Joe's Pizza, but it was still nice to be sitting there with Bobby. It feels like ages since we've had any time together. Another one of the Big Guy's tricks? Last year Bobby was my Biology partner. I got to know him and really like him. And I think he liked me. This year I hardly ever see him. Even at lunch. I know he's busy on the varsity football team, but that excuse is getting pretty old. So, are we not supposed to like each other anymore? Is that what you're telling me, Big Guy?

I tried to push the Big Guy out of my mind and concentrate on Bobby. He asked me how I was doing.

"Fine," I said. "How are you doing?"

"Fine."

Bobby and I sat there in silence for a bit. "How's football?" I asked, just to keep the conversation going.

Bobby started telling me about the game last week. He was excited because he caught a long pass for a touchdown.

"That's great!" I said.

"Yeah. My first varsity touchdown for Latin!"

I raised the can of Coke I was drinking. "Go Bobby! Here's to more touchdowns!"

"Thanks." Bobby raised the soda he was drinking, and we clinked cans.

"I'm really happy for you," I said. "Latin's hero."

"Thanks," Bobby said again, though I could see he was a little embarrassed by my compliments.

Was he blushing? Remembering what had happened in the woods, I had a sudden urge to touch his face. I wondered if Bobby would ever let me do that again.

There was another small moment of silence as Bobby looked away from me and focused on his sandwich. "So, what's new with you?" he asked, still chewing on his food.

"Nothing much," I answered. "I'm studying hard, waiting for my PSAT scores, trying to stay out of trouble." I told him about the Halloween party. "I wish you'd been there. We had a great time."

"Yeah, I heard." Bobby looked away again. "I—I was tired. Practice takes a lot of out of me, so I need to rest."

"Yeah, I guess it does."

"Sorry I wasn't there though. It sounds like it was good."

"Yeah, it was." I told him about what Mr. Felucci said. That the teachers would help us out with anything we were doing on climate change.

Bobby nodded. "That's great."

Why did I get the feeling Bobby was just nodding to agree with me? That his mind was on other things and he didn't care one way or the other what I was saying?

We were silent again. Bobby finished his sandwich, cleaned up his area, and stood up suddenly. "Gotta go, RV. I'm late. Nice to catch up with you."

"Yeah. Good to catch up."

"See you soon." He turned back around as he was leaving. "At another game maybe?"

"Yeah, sure."

And he was gone.

I felt more and more depressed as he walked away. I've never spent any time with Bobby that felt so awkward. Not knowing what to say to each other? When did that happen to Bobby and me? What did it mean?

Something definitely has changed in our friendship. And it makes me very sad. And I don't know what to do about it. I suppose Mr. Aniso would tell me I need to talk to Bobby. Do I have the guts to do that? What would I say? And what would Bobby say back? Just thinking about that gets me so scared.

*

I went to Joe's for lunch today, needing to gather my thoughts. Saturdays are good. Mom and Dad haven't been pressuring me too much about finding a job or doing too many errands on weekends. They're into the study-and-get-good-grades thing. "Let's see how the school year goes," they've told me, making sure I know good grades are Pressure Number One. I can deal with it. I know they worry about money, but so far, they take those worries out on each other, not me. I should be thankful for that.

I was glad to see Mark at Joe's. I guess more and more people are discovering it. Okay. Mark's becoming a friend, so I'm happy to share my hideaway with him.

"Can I sit down?" I asked Mark.

"Sure."

"What are you having?"

"Just a plain slice."

"Want another one?"

"Naw. I'm okay."

I went up to the counter to order my own slice. Joe poked his head from behind the ovens.

"Hey, RV! How's my Latin scholar?"

"Doing okay," I said. "Just trying to keep up with everything."

"Just okay? A smart kid like you?" Joe teased. "I'm waiting for you to be doing great, so you can give me your autograph."

I smiled. Joe had a way of making me feel good, no matter what he said. He asked me what I wanted and then pointed to a pizza on the counter. "How about the Crunchy Calamari slice? That's today's special."

I made a face. "Fish on pizza? No way. How about a slice of pepperoni and a Coke?"

Joe shook his head. "Okay, RV. Have it your way." He winked at me as he gave me my slice. "But wait till I get famous and all these slices go up in price. Then you'll wish you had tried them when they were cheap!"

Laughing, I took my food and went back to Mark. "Joe's a good guy," I said, sitting down. "He always makes me laugh."

Mark tried to smile but I could see he wasn't that into it. I wondered if he came to Joe's, like I did, when he was feeling down or needed to sort something out.

"Tim and Carole's party was great, wasn't it?" I said, trying to think of something good to talk about.

Mark nodded. "Yeah, it was nice. All those great costumes."

"Weren't they though? Makes me hope Tim and Carole have another party."

Mark nodded again but didn't say anything, taking another few bites of his pizza slice.

I flashed back to my lunch with Bobby. Oh-oh. Not another awkward meal. I came to Joe's to sort out my own thoughts about Bobby and other stuff. I wasn't going to have to wonder about Mark now, was I?"

I tried again. "Hey, maybe we can try to throw a party," I suggested, half joking.

"It would be a disaster," Mark said. "I'm no good at anything like that."

I could see he was not in a mood for jokes. "Hey, Mark. Are you okay?" I finally asked.

"Yeah. Why?"

"I don't know. You just seem down. I come to Joe's when I feel down. Is that why you come here too?"

Mark thought for a while. He started to shake his head, but then stopped. "Well, there is something. Something that's bothering me."

"Yeah?"

"Yeah." He looked down at the table, squirming a little bit, and then looked back up at me. "It has to do with you."

"Me?"

"Yeah."

I waited for him to continue.

"You know that demonstration that's going on about the gay teacher?" he began.

I nodded.

"Someone saw you there last week."

"I was coming home from a movie in town, and I saw Mr. Aniso there," I explained. "So, we talked for a while."

"Yeah, I know you're friends."

Mark looked as uncomfortable as I felt. We both were looking up, down, and around, anywhere but at each other. Finally, Mark looked at me and said, "Are—are you gay?"

"I'm—I'm—maybe. I'm not totally sure. I get so confused sometimes."

First Bobby. Then Carole. And now Mark. I'm glad I didn't say no. But I wish I could have said something more definite. Though beats me what that would have been.

Mark was quiet, looking down at the table and thinking. "Does it bother you?" I finally blurted out. My heart was beating furiously. How would I respond if he said yes?

Mark shook his head. "No."

"No?"

"No."

I relaxed a little. Mark was still quiet. I felt myself blushing. Why did everything have to be such a big deal?

"My brother's gay," Mark said suddenly.

"Your brother?"

"My older brother, Simon. He's in college."

If Mark had a brother who was gay, he would understand about these things, I told myself.

But Mark said, "It was terrible."

"What?"

"It was terrible when Simon came out last year. I told you my folks are really religious. They can't accept him. Especially my father. They had a horrible fight and my father threatened to cut him off and not pay for school."

My heart was beating loudly as I imagined what such a scene would be like in my family.

"That's too bad," was all I could think of to say. "Are things any better now?"

"Not really. He's cut himself off from the family. He rarely talks to us, mostly to my mother. My mother has convinced my father not to stop paying his tuition. But she's still after Simon to change, so they fight about that when they do talk." He looked up at me again. "And now my parents are putting more pressure on me."

"On you?"

"Yeah. To toe the line in everything. Be the perfect Christian. It's really hard some days."

"I'm sorry," I mumbled, trying to take in everything he was telling me. Did that explain why he looked so sad so often?

I tried to think of something to comfort him. "I wish parents knew how much pressure they put on their kids," I finally said. I was thinking about Bobby and my family too.

Mark was nodding. "Yeah. It really sucks."

Mark never swore. So, I knew he was very upset.

"I'm sorry to lay all this on you." He turned to me. "It's just that last night was another bad fight."

Where had I heard that before?

"It's okay," I said, trying to comfort him. I tried to make a little joke. "That's what Joe's is for. It's like adults drowning their sorrows in bars with drink. We drown our sorrows with pizza."

Mark let out a little laugh, and I was happy to see that.

We talked some more. I told Mark a little bit more about my life and the pressures my parents laid on me about being part of the immigrant community. I told him what a hard time I had getting out of going to Lith camp this past summer.

That made Mark really laugh. "And I got out of going to Christian camp this summer!"

I laughed too. It feels so good when you find out someone is going through the same things you are, even when the things are bad.

When we finally stood up to leave, I had to ask, "So—so if I am gay, that doesn't bother you? I know how born-again Christians are."

Mark shook his head. "Not all born-again Christians. Don't stereotype."

I apologized. But Mark wasn't upset. He told me he was glad we had our talk. Then to my surprise he gave me a big hug.

"Thanks," he said.

"Thanks," I said back.

*

I'm having a hard time sleeping. So, I told Mark I might be gay. No big deal, right? His brother's gay, he understands. So, what's bothering me?

I don't know. Why does it feel like every time I reveal what's going on inside me, it's so scary? Haven't I learned that people like me better for it? At least some people. Carole. Mr. Aniso. And maybe Bobby. Though he wasn't very happy when I admitted I told Mr. Aniso about him and me. That was bad. But it bugs me sometimes that Bobby is so adamant about keeping our secret.

Adamant. A good word. Maybe I'm adamant about talking about what's going on inside me. At least sometimes. So that does mean Bobby and I are growing apart? I'm adamant one way and Bobby is adamant the opposite way. Is that why I haven't seen more of him this year? That makes me incredibly sad.

I'm not sure what love is exactly, but I know I still care about Bobby. So much. And the few times we've touched each other... Man, that jolt of electricity that went through my whole body was amazing. When that happens between two people, does that mean it's love? If it does, then Bobby and I love each other. Or should I put that in the past?

I can't lose Bobby as a friend. I just can't. It's bad enough that Carole is spending so much time with Mr. Computer-Genius-Turned-Climate-Genius Tim. And when she's not with Tim, she's still swooning about her French guy, François. Figuring out friendships sure is crazy. I've got to stop these negative thoughts.

Didn't I just have a good, honest conversation with Mark? We might become better friends because of it, right? I like him. So, all that's good, right? What was that line I heard in that movie? "When God closes a door, somewhere He opens a window." It's cliché, but maybe there's a reason why clichés exist. Maybe they're true. At least sometimes.

*

What would Dr. Freud make of this dream? Mark and Miss Sánchez came to my house for dinner. Miss Sánchez was looking even more gorgeous than usual. She was wearing a tight red sweater, making her breasts look even bigger than they do in class. I was totally embarrassed when she sat down at the table. I tried not to look at her but kept glancing her way anyway. Ray, though, was totally mesmerized. That made me mad, and I reminded Ray that he should stick with his nice new girlfriend, Roberta. Ray shot back that he could have as many girlfriends as he wanted. That I should stop being jealous. I told him I wasn't jealous, but he said I was. While we were arguing, Mark was having a great time laughing and joking with Mom and Dad. That made me mad too. Ray started laughing, asking if I was jealous of Mark too. Then a crazy thing happened. Ray and Miss Sánchez started making out right there at the table. She told him he was getting an A. I asked what about me? She ignored me, and I began panicking. Then I woke up.

Man, what does that all mean? Everyone's ignoring me in my dreams. Why? And why would Ray kissing Miss Sánchez make me panic? How can I be jealous?

I should stop trying to make sense of my crazy dreams and concentrate on school. That reminds me, I have a Spanish quiz later today. I was going to study more for it last night, but I didn't. Is that what's really bothering me? Would Miss Sánchez give me a better grade if I paid more attention to her? Is that what I'm really worried about? Maybe dreams do mean something, just in a different way.

Chapter Eight

Bad News

"RV, what's the Pythagorean Theorem?"

"Um, it has to do with the triangle."

"What about the triangle?"

"It's—it's a right triangle."

"What does that mean?"

"It means—it means the sides are the same?"

Mr. Felucci, our math teacher, turned away from me. "Mark? What's a right triangle?"

"One angle is ninety degrees."

"And the theorem?"

"It says that the square of the hypotenuse is equal to the squares of the other two sides."

Mr. Felucci turned back to me.

"You got that, RV? You should know that by now. Please repeat it."

I repeated what Mark said, wanting to shrink a little lower in my seat. Mr. Felucci might be fun at parties, but he goes back to his drill-sergeant self in class. Whenever he calls on me everything I've learned just flies out of my head. Not that math penetrates my thick skull for long anyway. I thought geometry might be fun, what with measuring things, but it's getting harder than I thought. Or else it's my brain that's at fault or Mr. Felucci's teaching.

Luckily, Mark's in the same class. After the class ended, he told me he'd be happy to help me with math if I ever needed it. My other math whiz, Carole, is rarely able to help me these days. She's taken up with other subjects, like Tim and François, ha ha. I'll be glad to take Mark's help. Someone's looking out for me.

I didn't have such a good time in some other classes today, including Latin, where I got screeched at by Miss Wagstaff. So, I went to Joe's for a pick-me-up slice after school. And what do I see? A big sign next to the door: SPACE FOR RENT. And there was a phone number to call to ask about renting.

I walked right up to the counter and sought out Joe. I asked him about the sign.

He nodded, not looking like his cheery, teasing self. "It's the rent." He made a motion with his finger to show it was going up, way up.

"What a bummer," I said. "You can't do anything about it?"

"I've been negotiating with the landlord for weeks, RV. But no go."

The look on my face must have been really bad because he then he quickly said, "Don't worry, RV. I'm looking for a new place."

"You are?"

"Yeah. It's not easy. But God willing, I'll find one."

"Okay." I nodded, not knowing what else to say. Joe's, gone? I was having a hard time absorbing the information.

"RV, RV, it's okay," Joe said. "It's not hopeless. I have a few leads."

I appreciated Joe trying to make me feel better, but I still stood there like a dummy, not saying anything.

Joe went to the glass case where different pizzas were laid out, took out a slice, and handed it to me. "Here," he said. "This is on the house today. This will make you feel better."

"What is it?" I asked, looking at all the stuff on top.

"My Ricotta Surprise."

"What's that?"

Joe was laughing and shaking his head at the same time. "RV, don't make such a face. You'll like it. It's a little ricotta cheese, roasted pear slices, caramelized onions, and balsamic vinaigrette for a little extra tang." I must still have looked doubtful because he went on, "I know how you hate vegetables on pizza. There's not a vegetable on it. Just try it."

"Onions are a vegetable, aren't they?" I said.

Joe tried to look annoyed. "C'mon, RV. I know you like onions. Caramelized onions are delicious. Give it a try. *Mangia! Mangia!*"

I got a Coke and took the slice back to a booth.

I looked at the slice and bit into it. Joe was right. It wasn't bad. As a matter of fact, it was really good.

"Thanks, Joe," I yelled out from my seat. "It is good!"

Joe gave me a thumbs-up sign and went back to his work as I hungrily took more bites.

After I finished my slice, I said a little prayer, right there in the booth. I asked The Big Guy to help Joe find a new place. I don't know if that's on the Big Guy's To-Do List, but if it wasn't, I told Him to add it. Then I realized I needed a bit of forgiveness.

"Yeah. Yeah. I know I just think about you when I need you. So, I'm sorry about that. If you do exist, you'll understand, Big Guy. I'm human. I'm fifteen years old. I'm not perfect. But I need a good pizza place to deal with life. I can put up with a lot of crap, only if there's a Joe's to go back to. So please, don't turn a deaf ear for once. This is really important."

Sometimes I feel stupid for praying. It's like those people who walk down the street, talking to someone invisible. Is that what I'm doing? But then people like

Mom say that's the whole point. Praying is slowly opening yourself up to the Big Guy. That He's always there, we just don't see Him. That it's not about talking to Him, but letting Him start talking to us, which we do by praying. It's a sign of hope.

Is that why I still do it? It's good to have hope, right? Even when things are bad, it's good to believe deep down they will get better.

I sat there at Joe's not wanting to leave. Whatever else happened in school today had flown out of my head. It didn't matter and seemed puny in comparison to the news Joe had told me. Funny how life can change your attitude. Life might want to take Joe's Pizza away from me, but I'm not going to let it do that without a fight. Is that what hope gives you?

*

When I went to the dinner table, Mom and Dad were in a heated discussion about the merger of the churches here in West Roxbury and the new construction.

Dad said he hoped the judge would rule in the churches' favor.

Mom said she hoped not, even though she couldn't believe she was saying that.

Dad said the church had a right to decide what to do.

Mom said they were doing it out of desperation because they needed money. *"Bažnyčioms reikia pinigų."*

Dad said the church would get some money out of the deal. And besides, the new construction would create a lot of jobs, giving a lot of other people an opportunity to make money. Including maybe even him. *"Bet bus daugiau žmonėms darbų. Gal ir aš susirasiu geresnį darbą."*

Ray and I turned our heads from one to the other. It felt like a ping-pong match. Mom was still against the deal, saying the merger wasn't good in the long run for a lot of reasons. Dad was for the merger.

There's a big demonstration planned for later in the week to try to influence the judge. Ray asked if Mom and Dad were going to go. They both said yes. Funny how things work. Dad, the agnostic, was siding with the churches. Mom, who's so religious, was against them. She said she had even given some money to the organization that had brought the lawsuit to stop the merger in the first place.

They continued talking. For a while, it seemed like a discussion rather than an argument. Though with Mom and Dad you never know when it becomes personal. Neither one changed their opinion. Toward the end of the discussion, Dad insisted the new construction would create jobs, one of which he would be happy to get. Mom told him he shouldn't just think of himself. That tearing down one church would cut services for a lot of people who needed it. And so, it got into argument territory again.

Ray and I managed to finish our food and left the dinner table before things got any worse. I went to my room, lay down on my bed, and started thinking about Joe's Pizza again. Some things were worth fighting for, weren't they? Didn't I feel as strongly about Joe's Pizza disappearing the way Mom and Dad felt about the church merger and construction project?

"What's the matter?"

"What?"

Ray was standing in my doorway. Well, that was a switch. Ray coming to check on how I was doing? When did he start caring about me? He asked me again what the matter was.

"Nothing," I said, still in shock that he was standing there. "Why do you ask?"

"You have that frown on your face. And you looked like that all through dinner."

"I was just hoping Mom and Dad's argument wouldn't turn worse."

"You mean like it usually does?"

"Yeah."

"So. What's so different about today?"

We both listened for a minute. Mom and Dad had finally stopped talking. Someone was putting dishes into the sink. So, the discussion hadn't turned worse. Dinner was over without a big fight.

Ray started turning around to leave.

"Actually, there is something on my mind," I said.

Ray turned back. "What?"

I told him about Joe's Pizza closing.

"So. He'll find another space somewhere."

"How do you know?"

"People usually do." He shrugged. "Besides, if he doesn't, there are a million other pizza places to go to." And with that, he left.

I didn't move from my bed. Ray didn't care about Joe's Pizza. But I did. What if I started a demonstration so it wouldn't close? Didn't I care strongly enough about it?

I laughed at myself. How many people would I get? Maybe Carole. Maybe Mark. Probably not Bobby. Anyone else from school? Mr. Aniso? That was about it. I remembered the dream I had about Dad making us march in front of City Hall. Yeah, it would be like that. Me turning into Dad? No way!

But then I got a better idea. Didn't Joe say he already had some leads for new spaces? I told myself I would go to Joe's and ask him if he needed any help with finding a new place. I had no idea what I could do, but you never know, do you? I care enough about Joe's, just like Mom and Dad care about the proposed church merger. I might not be able to organize a demonstration, but if there is any way I can help him out, I'll do it.

*

"Hi, RV."

"Oh, hi, Mr. Aniso."

"I thought I might find you here. How are you doing?"

"Fine," I answered.

I pointed to the sign in the window and told Mr. Aniso I had come by to offer my help to Joe as he was looking for a new space.

"That's very nice of you," Mr. Aniso said. He asked if I'd mind if he got a slice and sat with me for a few minutes.

"Sure. That's fine."

"I haven't seen you in ages," Mr. Aniso said, sitting down in my booth after he got his slice. "It's nice to catch up. I miss our chats."

"Yeah," I answered, nodding. "Me too."

"How have you been?"

"Okay."

Mr. Aniso smiled and turned his head a little to one side, as if he was a doctor examining me. "Are you sure?" he asked, pointing his finger at my head and twirling it around. "I see a lot of thoughts spinning around in there. They're good thoughts, I hope."

I smiled too. It's always good to see Mr. Aniso, even when I don't know what to say to him. He makes me feel like more of an adult. But then I don't always think I'm acting like one.

I told him Joe appreciated my offer, and if he thought of anything, he'd let me know.

"I even offered to start a demonstration to have the landlord lower the rent," I added. "But Joe told me it was too late for that." I shook my head. "So, at this point, I'm just waiting. I hate waiting!"

Mr. Aniso tried to calm me down as always. "Yes, waiting is hard. Sometimes it's all we can do. Other times, we find out there are things we can do."

"Yeah, I guess so." I didn't really want to be calmed down.

Then I felt myself blush.

"Yes?" Mr. Aniso said.

"Joe also told me he has a few leads," I admitted. "He said he'd try to find a nice, homey space where I and my friends could come relax and work out anything that was bothering us." I laughed despite myself. "How does he know I like to do that here?"

"Isn't it obvious?" Mr. Aniso smiled again. "What better place to work out life's problems than Joe's Pizza, right?"

We both laughed. How true that was. Mr. Aniso sure knows me, maybe even better than I know myself. Joe too. No wonder I like to come here.

Mr. Aniso asked me how my friends were doing.

"Carole is spending a lot of time with Tim. I think they're going out. Though I don't know what she'll do when her French friend François comes to visit for the holidays."

"And Bobby?" Mr. Aniso asked.

"Oh, Bobby. I hardly see him. Ever since he made the varsity team, he's feeling the pressure to do well." I told Mr. Aniso how nervous I was when he was hurt at that game I went to with Mark. I wanted to change the subject. "But I'm getting friendlier with Mark," I said, trying to get us back to a cheerier topic. "He's a nice guy. We've begun to hang around together." I recounted to Mr. Aniso what Mark had told me about his brother being gay and his religious parents being upset about it. "So, you can see he has his pressures too."

"Yes, it's sad how coming out is still so difficult for so many people." Mr. Aniso nodded. "Especially for people from religious families."

I nodded, too, remembering what Mr. Aniso had told me about his own background and what happened to him at the seminary. I wondered how much of it applied to me.

Mr. Aniso finished his slice and looked at his watch. "Oh, RV. I have to run. I was in the neighborhood and decided to stop in here in case you were here. And you were! But please, I meant what I said about missing our talks. Please feel free to text me if you ever want to talk about anything. Or just say hi and catch up, like we did today. Okay?" He shook his head. "I said I'd never say it again, but I am. Never feel like you're bothering me."

Again, I thought he was about to grab my shoulder the way he did when he wanted to emphasize how serious he was about something. But he didn't today.

Mr. Aniso stood up and gathered his things, ready to leave. "Oh," I said, remembering something. "How's that teacher doing? The one you were demonstrating about?"

He shook his head. "The judge said the school had a right to fire him. He said they have their beliefs and have a right to employ people who share their beliefs."

"Just for his beliefs?" I asked. "That doesn't seem fair. People all have their beliefs."

Mr. Aniso nodded. "Yes. But the judge said that wasn't the point. The point was that the school had a right to hire and fire who they wanted to. That if they felt someone was damaging their reputation, they had a right to fire that person."

"What are you guys going to do about it?"

Mr. Aniso shrugged. "I don't know yet. There's talk of an appeal, and people are talking to lawyers to determine how strong the case is. Though Mr. Briggs isn't sure he wants to continue fighting."

I was trying to process that bit of information when Mr. Aniso came up to me. "Don't worry, RV. We're still fighting for him. Even if he stops the fight, we won't." There was that hand on my shoulder. It was a light touch, not hard like usual. "If you believe that something is wrong, you don't give up trying to change it, do you?"

I shook my head. "No, you don't."

"Never," he said. "You never give up. You have to have hope. Changing things can take a long time. But they can change." And with that he took his hand away, turned around, and walked out of Joe's.

Chapter Nine

Thanksgiving Blues

"It will be great if you can come, RV."

"Okay."

"No, really. This will be such a great game, and if I know you're there, it will be that much better."

Bobby was urging me to go to the Thanksgiving Day football game between Latin and English High School. Hard to believe the rivalry has been going on since 1887. Latin School has been winning most of the games for about the last fifty years, so I'm not sure they need my support. But it's important to Bobby. He said he's back full force since he had to limp off the field a couple of weeks ago, and he'll be starting for Latin once again.

We're going to our snooty cousins, the S-heads, for Thanksgiving dinner later that day, so I told Bobby I'd have to check with Mom and Dad. Someone would have to drive me to Harvard Stadium for the game, and then I'd have to come back in time to go to the S-heads'.

Bobby said he understood and hoped I'd be able to work things out. Then we hung up without making any other plans. I'm glad Bobby called, though it was the first time he called me in I don't know how long. I'm trying not to think this way, but I can't help thinking he only calls me when he needs something. Is that fair? It certainly seems like it this fall.

But I'll try to be at the game to support Bobby. If nothing else, it will show him that I still care about him. And I keep telling myself that things will change after football. Yeah, Bobby plays on other teams, too, but they're junior varsity, not varsity. So maybe he won't feel he has to prove anything. And he'll have time for his friends. Not like with football, anyway.

There's that word again. Hope. I'm being hopeful, aren't I? Well, maybe it's good. Better than being cynical and giving up, isn't it?

*

Neither Mark nor Carole could go to watch Latin play football, being busy with their own Thanksgiving Day plans. But Dad of all people said he'd drive me. Not only that, he'd go to the game with me. Then we'd drive back home and pick up Mom and Ray in time to go to the S-heads for dinner.

Not very often that Dad and I do things together. Not sure why, but it just doesn't happen. So, there we were sitting in Harvard Stadium together. It felt a little weird, but if Dad was trying to bond with me, I needed to give him the chance, right? I reminded myself I'm hopeful RV these days, not the other one, ha ha.

At least there was one thing Dad and I could bond on. He knows about as much about football as I do. I told him I'd explain things to him as the game went along. Dad said okay. I couldn't help chuckling to myself. Me, explaining football to someone. Well, I did learn a few things from Mark, I reminded myself. But then I also remembered Bobby had promised to take me to a Patriots game. That hadn't happened. Was it ever going to?

I tried to put that thought out of my head when they introduced the players. I pointed out Bobby to Dad.

Dad told me I should invite him to dinner again. That he was a nice guy. "*Geras vyrukas.*" "A good young man."

"*Taip.*" "Yeah" was about all I could say, thinking about so many things I dared not mention to Dad.

It was cold, and I was glad I remembered to bring some snacks and something warm to drink. As we were munching on some peanuts, I tried to explain the difference between offense and defense in the game, as best as I knew how. Dad was nodding, though I'm not sure he really understood. Can't blame the guy. I'm not sure if my explanation made sense. For all I know, I could have gotten things reversed.

As expected, Latin started off well and looked like they were on their way to win again, easily. I looked around and this time I did spot Bobby's parents, sitting down front, waving pennants and cheering Latin on. It was fun to cheer with everybody else when Latin did well. At halftime, the score was Latin 14, English 12.

"Go Wolfpack!" I yelled as loud as anybody as the players came out on the field for the third quarter. Latin scored again. The crowd really got going when a few plays later Bobby caught a long pass from the quarterback and started running toward the end zone. If he scored a touchdown, we knew there'd be no stopping Latin.

Bobby was running, I was cheering, Dad was cheering, Bobby's parents were cheering, thousands of people were cheering. Suddenly two English players caught up with him and tackled him. Bobby flopped down onto the ground and stayed there.

The cheering stopped, and other cheering and clapping started by people who supported English. But then the entire crowd got quieter as Bobby didn't move. I started to hear anxious murmurs as a couple of players and officials gathered around Bobby.

Dad wondered how badly he was hurt.

I told him I wondered the same thing.

Although I couldn't see Bobby any longer because of the crowd of people around him, it still didn't look like he was getting up. The next thing I knew, a couple of guys came out with a stretcher, put Bobby on it, and carried him off the field.

I saw Bobby's parents rush out of their seats, making their way to where they took Bobby. I wanted to do the same, but I knew the officials probably wouldn't let me see him. I tried to calm myself down by promising to call his parents as soon as I got home. But I feared the worst. The two guys who tackled him hit him pretty hard. If he was hurt badly... I tried not to think about it.

The game continued after a while, but I was hardly paying attention, my mind totally fixated on Bobby. Latin School won, but I didn't care.

As we were leaving, Dad made a comment that basketball was a better sport, saying people didn't get hurt like in football. Couldn't disagree there, not at that moment. But then Dad got on his Old Country diatribe. He said he hoped Bobby was all right, but then he kept on about basketball, reminding me that basketball is the national sport of Lithuania. And how it's more humane. And why couldn't the US be more humane?

Dad's chattering really got on my nerves. "Why don't you be more humane!" I wanted to shout. "Can't you see I don't care about basketball? I care about Bobby!" I told him as much, though in gentler language. Only in slightly gentler language. That made Dad shut up. We drove home the rest of the way in silence. I could tell he was frustrated his bonding opportunity with his son didn't work out the way he wanted it to. Sorry about that. But couldn't he see things from my perspective and understand how important it was for me to find out how Bobby was doing?

I called Bobby's cell and his house from the car and again when we got home. No one answered. Mom and

Dad could see that I was upset and tried to cheer me up by saying Bobby would be okay.

I just shrugged, not wanting to play along and not feeling in a Thanksgiving Day mood. What was there to be thankful for?

*

I finally got through on Bobby's cell as we were driving to the S-heads' house for dinner. It was his mother who picked up the phone. She told me they were there with Bobby in the hospital. Bobby was conscious, but he was banged up pretty badly. No one was sure yet, but it looked like Bobby had suffered a bad concussion. The doctors were going to do some tests to confirm it. But at least he wasn't paralyzed, she told me. I thought I heard her stifle a cry.

I thanked Bobby's mother and asked her to call me when she had some news. She promised she would.

I shut off the phone and stared out of the car window. A concussion was bad, but it wasn't as bad as other ways I feared Bobby could be injured. After that I could relax a little bit. I sighed, watching woods and hills pass by as we made our way to the S-heads' house. I wished I could be there in the woods, relaxing and by myself, instead of making inane chitchat with the S-heads at Thanksgiving Day dinner. (Inane. Great word. It means stupid, but in a polite way. The way many people behave at these social functions, pretending everything is hunky-dory, while ignoring what is really happening in the world around them.)

We got to the S-heads' house, and sure enough, as soon as we all sat down to dinner, the inane conversations started. I love it. Here we go again. A mini United Nations with the S-heads. The kids talk in English, the parents talk in the Mother Tongue, and no one's paying attention to anyone else. Mr. S-head and Dad began talking about the Russians and the Chinese and how the Americans weren't doing enough to counteract their power. Mom and Mrs. S-head talked about Lithuanian and immigrant affairs. The kids talked about movies and TV shows and dances.

But then the parents' talk turned to what the kids were doing. Of course, the two S-head kids were the stars of the show. Cousin Jolanda is a year younger than me but is on her way to being a big-time model. She's already had some photo shoots in magazines. Even I can see she's even more gorgeous this year than last year, so I can't resent her for her looks. Ray, of course, is even more mesmerized by her.

Funny how that works. I kept glancing over at Ray, and I could see he's just as mesmerized by Jolanda as I am by Bobby. When you meet a particular person, it's like something takes over you, and your whole being is focused on that person. You're drawn to them like a magnet. The magnet is powerful, and you can't pull away. Even though Ray seems happy with his new girlfriend, Roberta, and has been acting so different, he couldn't take his eyes off Jolanda the minute we arrived. The guy is definitely mesmerized.

And Jonas, well, Jonas is the superstar. He's now a senior and, of course, has applied for early acceptance at

Harvard. He hasn't heard yet, but is there any question that he'll get in? His surgeon daddy has money, and probably has already made a donation to Harvard to help little Jonas secure his place there. Okay, okay. I'm getting cynical again. His grades are good, as his parents keep pointing out, but I bet having money doesn't hurt.

Of course, his parents like to pretend that money doesn't matter. Talk turned to all the extracurricular activities Jonas is involved in. He's in the National Honor Society, he's a Super-Lith, and he's active in organizations in the fancy prep school he goes to. How he does it, I have no idea.

Sure enough, though, someone asked me about the extracurricular activities I'm involved in.

"Ah, well, nothing at the moment. I'm just trying to keep up my grades in school and figure out my crush on Bobby." Wouldn't it be great if I could just say that?

But no. I hemmed and hawed and focused on the good-grades thing.

Of course, then everyone jumped on me saying that good grades were not enough. Jonas reminded me that it's important for colleges to see extracurricular activities throughout high school and that I better start sophomore year if I haven't already.

Mrs. S-head got on her immigrant high horse and suggested I join the Lith clubs Jonas was involved in. She turned to Jonas and asked him if he'd take me under his wing.

Oh, great. I want that so much. To be under the wing of my older, super-confident cousin, who gets me drunk at Lith events and causes me to throw up.

Even Mom threw her two cents in. She reminded me how Jonas used to do the readings at Lith church when he was younger. And the others joined in.

"Gal tu gali skaityti skaitymus, Arvydai?"

"Jo. Žinau kad gražiai skaitai lietuviškai kaip mano Jonas."

"Labai lengva, Arvydai. Jeigu mano brolis gali, tu gali."

"Why can't you do the readings, RV?"

"Yes. I know you read Lithuanian as well as my Jonas."

"It's very easy, RV. If my brother can do it, so can you."

I tried to wriggle out of it, but in the end was forced to say I'd think about it. I wonder if that's how a delegate to the UN feels when the whole world is trying to force you to admit your country is doing something bad. Bamboozled. Where did I pick up that word? Who cares? All I know is that's how I felt at Thanksgiving Day dinner.

Oh, well. At least we got through without any major arguments. After everyone got through bamboozling me, talk turned to the other usual things like upcoming social events in the Lith community and gossip about people's cholesterol, arthritis, and affairs.

All the bamboozling had given me indigestion and I couldn't eat much of my turkey. I told Mom and Dad it was because I was worried about Bobby, which was partly true. I told them I'd be able to eat more later when I calmed down and found out more news about how Bobby was doing.

After the dinner, we all got a tour of Mrs. S-head's kitchen. She has redone it, so as we walked through, we made more inane comments, complimenting her on the colorful granite countertops, the shiny new chrome, and the expensive-looking cappuccino maker and other gadgets.

Yup, the S-heads have a lot to be thankful for. If I let Mom, Dad and the S-heads have their way, I'll soon learn to follow their example.

Chapter Ten

The Spanish Club

Funny how great minds think alike. Or at least minds of people who are becoming good friends.

"Would you like to join Miss Sánchez's Spanish club with me?" Mark asked me one afternoon.

"Funny you should ask," I said.

"Why?"

"I've been thinking I need to join a club or two." I told Mark about the bamboozling I received at Thanksgiving Day dinner.

Mark laughed. "You too?" He told me talk at his house has been about the cost of college, and he is also feeling the pressure to do whatever he can to increase his chances of getting a scholarship or financial aid.

I shook my head. I was laughing, too, though it wasn't a very happy laugh. "Whatever happened to enjoying your sophomore year? I thought we were supposed to start thinking about college next year."

Mark nodded. "Ha! Next year is supposed to be the serious one with SATs and all that. But you know how it is. Some parents start worrying about it in kindergarten." He was silent for a second and then added, "I'm not a big joiner, but I've been thinking I don't want to be left behind. So, if we do something together, I'm game."

"But will Miss Sánchez let us in the Spanish club?" I asked. "It's December. Maybe they don't allow late joiners. Shows we're laggards."

Mark punched me playfully in the arm. "Laggards? We're not laggards! We'll think of an excuse. A positive excuse!"

"Like what?"

"Like, I don't know."

*

Miss Sánchez couldn't have been nicer about letting us into the Spanish club. Mark forced me to do the talking for both of us. I made up some lame excuse about hard classes like chemistry and math, which took all our time at the beginning of the year. I also remembered something that Carole had taught me about negotiating when we were in the computer fix-it business together. To be nice and complimentary when trying for new business. So, I added that Mark and I really enjoyed Spanish class, wanted to learn more about Spain, and that Miss Sánchez was our favorite teacher.

Boy, did I lay it on thick. Go, RV! You can come through with the BS as well as anybody! Is it the influence of Thanksgiving Day dinner with the S-heads? (Sorry, Big Guy. You'll forgive my BS, won't you? You know Mr. Aniso is still my favorite all-time teacher.)

There I go again, praying about petty stuff. Wasn't I just telling myself about listening to the Big Guy instead of babbling away at Him? When am I going to learn to do that? Now? So, what's He saying? Nothing so far.

Miss Sánchez said she'd be happy to have both of us in the club. Maybe that was the Big Guy's answer. The only rule was that we should talk Spanish as best we could. No English allowed. I can deal with that.

We get together on Tuesday afternoons after classes, and today was our first day.

"*¡Hola!* Mark, RV," Miss Sánchez said when we entered the room. "*demos todos la bienvenida a los nuevos miembros de nuestro club.*" I figured she'd said welcome new members, because all the kids started saying hello.

"*¡Hola!*" both Mark and I said. There are about a dozen people in the club. No one I know, but some of whom I recognize by sight. They all seem nice though. No Duffy or Doyle types. Not that I expected them to come to something like this, but you never know.

Miss Sánchez told us our timing was good, making us feel even better. She explained that in the beginning of the semester, the club had concentrated on learning about some basic Spanish greetings and culture. Now they were starting to talk geography and travel.

Great, travel, I thought. My cup of tea. I want to travel everywhere when I get older. Mark and I made the right decision.

"*Mark, si pudieras visitar España, ¿a dónde te gustaría ir primero?*" she asked as we were sitting down. "If you could visit Spain, where would you like to go first?"

I saw Mark blush a little as he tried to come up with an answer, saying he wasn't sure. "*Um, um, no estoy seguro.*"

"*¿No estás seguro?*" Miss Sánchez asked. But she was smiling while she said that. She went up to Mark, so that she was standing almost right over him. "*Vamos, Mark. Conoces algunas ciudades de España.*" Her eyes were twinkling, and she looked like she was having fun teasing him, saying that he must know some cities in Spain.

Mark blushed even more.

"Man, her standing over me like that got me totally discombobulated," Mark said after the club meeting was over and we were leaving to go home.

"Discombobulated. I didn't know you liked ten-cent words," I teased.

Mark ignored my teasing. He turned to me. "Did you see how gorgeous she looked today?"

"She always looks gorgeous."

"Yeah, but today, with that blue dress and those breasts right over me..." Mark looked so worked up he couldn't finish his sentence.

I was still laughing. "I didn't notice. But maybe when she stands over me sometime, I'll get discombobulated too," I teased again.

When we parted for home, I was still thinking about what Mark said. And I'm still thinking about him.

Yup, Mark is definitely mesmerized by Miss Sánchez. Just like Ray is mesmerized by Jolanda. And I enjoy seeing it.

Why? I'm not sure. Maybe it makes me feel less alone. I'm mesmerized, too, after all. By Bobby. But he's a guy, so that's different. Or is it?

What about Mark? I like him a lot, but am I mesmerized by him? I don't think so. It's certainly not the same as when I touched Bobby's cheek that time.

There I go again. All these questions. I've got to turn off that part of my brain and turn on the part that does homework. Great. No wonder it's so hard. Much more fun thinking about breasts, and kissing, and Bobby's cheek, than chemistry or Latin.

Come on, RV! You can think about the fun stuff later! I like being smart. I like going to Latin. And I like this new club, even if I feel bamboozled a little. So right now, let me get to work. Be one of those Latin scholars they're always talking about. The ones they always want us to look up to.

*

Oh, oh. I had another crazy dream. What's this one trying to tell me? I dreamed about fixing the computer at Mr. O'Malley's house, the first client Carole and I had when we started our fix-it business. But in the dream, instead of Carole, I was fixing the computer with Miss Sánchez. And just like with Carole, Miss Sánchez squeezed in behind Mr. Malley's desk to work with the wires. But she couldn't reach a couple.

"*Ayúdame, RV,*" she said. "*Ayúdame.*"

I didn't know people could speak foreign languages in your dreams, but there you have it. "Help me, RV!" she said. "Help me!"

So, I squeezed in beside her as best I could. And again, the same thing happened as with Carole. When I reached over to get a wire that was really hard to grasp, I jerked my body and fell right on top of Miss Sánchez. I could feel her breasts underneath me. I was so embarrassed. But Miss Sánchez started giggling. I tried to say, "I'm sorry," but since my mouth was so close to her body, the words came out muffled. Miss Sánchez continued giggling, enjoying herself, while I was getting more and more embarrassed, with those breasts right underneath mine. I tried to get up off her, but I couldn't. The more I tried, the more I was stuck to her. And then I woke up.

I could feel myself blushing. In the middle of the night, which doesn't surprise me anymore. What was that all about? Obviously, I notice Miss Sánchez's breasts like Mark does. How can you not? But does it mean I like them the way Mark does? He talks about them a lot when we're going home. To him they're magical and untouchable.

Are they magical and untouchable to me? Maybe. I mean, it was nice when I was lying there in the dream. But is nice the same as magical? Nice isn't magical, is it? And why haven't I dreamed about Bobby lately? Am I switching to Miss Sánchez when it comes to my dreams and sex? Or is this not about sex? What else could it be about? How could it be about anything else?

Man. Maybe I should think about studying psychology in college. I already have a lot of material to work with. Starting with my crazy brain.

*

Well, Mark's become a real friend. Being with him takes my mind off Bobby, at least for a little while. I've called and texted Bobby, but it's always his mother who picks up the phone or texts back. He's still in the hospital, which doesn't sound good. She says the concussion he had is worse than they at first thought, but she won't give me more precise information. Her excuse is that the doctors are still doing various tests, so she doesn't know more herself. I get the sense she's putting me off, though, which makes me feel bad. And she wants to get off the phone as fast as possible. That makes me feel worse.

I called Mr. Aniso once, but he didn't answer. I was going to leave him a message but then thought better of it.

There is nothing he can say to change the situation anyway. Carole was sympathetic when I talked to her about it, but there was only so much she could say too.

So at least Mark is there. He came over my house today. We went to Joe's and then spent the rest of the day in my favorite place in the woods. Never realized it before, but I suppose it's like an initiation rite I do. When someone means something special to me, I take them to these places. First Carole. Then Bobby. And now Mark. Since he lives so close by in Roslindale, it's not a big deal for him to come over.

Mark had one of his Christian Fellowship meetings in the morning, so he came over in the afternoon. We had to work on an essay for Spanish class. Not the best way to spend a Saturday afternoon, but not the worst either. Mark's a good guy, and I have fun teasing him because he gets so distracted in Spanish class.

"But Miss Sánchez is so beautiful," he keeps saying. "How can you even think of the *futuro simple* or other tenses when Miss Sánchez is standing there in front of you?"

I laugh. "You're becoming a dirty old man before your time," I tell him. He gets a little upset about that, but then I get him to laugh too.

Today, we had to write an essay about our families, using as many Spanish words as we could. Mine came out pretty well, I thought, and I helped Mark with his. And then Mark helped me with some chemistry equations I was having trouble with. Just half a year more, and then

I'm done with test tubes, hopefully forever. It's amazing how different people's brains are. Mark's brain is like Carole's, figuring out equations and math theorems as soon as they're taught to us. Me? Well, my brain tries to understand math and science, too, tries real hard, but it just doesn't get far. I feel like one of those rodents scientists make run on little treadmills in cages. My cage is Latin School. Running endlessly on the treadmill but staying in the same place is my brain. At least in math or chemistry.

After we finished our homework, I took Mark to Joe's Pizza to thank him for his help. I'm trying to go there as often as I can before Joe closes the place. I still can't believe it. I asked Joe if he made any progress on getting a new place. He put his fingers to his lips and said, "Shh. Don't jinx me."

That made me feel a little better, hoping that meant he was working on some kind of deal for a new Joe's. But I still felt a little sad looking around at the place. A lot of good memories and a lot of good conversations took place at Joe's. With Carole. With Bobby. And then with Mr. Aniso. A new place, no matter how nice, just wouldn't be the same.

"Why are you looking so sad?" Mark was staring at me, looking concerned.

"Oh, sorry," I said. "I'm just thinking about this place."

I told him about Joe's closing and about all my memories of the place.

Mark nodded. "Yeah, I get sad about things like that too." He told me about a little park he used to go near his house to read or just sit and think. "But now it's being cemented over for a parking lot. A parking lot!"

Mark told me his neighborhood doesn't have as many green spaces as mine. So, for him, he said, the disappearance of the park was a big deal.

"Hey, do you want to see a nice green space?" I asked.

"Sure," he said, looking at his watch. "I have time."

So, I took him to my special place in the woods.

"Wow!" he said. "This is great!"

"Yeah. I love it here."

We went to the big rock by the stream; the rock you can climb on and look out over the horizon. We sat there enjoying the view over the trees to the distant hills. It was cold, but there were only a few patches of snow on the grass. The bright sun had melted almost everything away. "Just looking up at the blue sky and puffy clouds makes me feel good about life," I said.

Mark bundled himself further into his jacket. "You're so lucky," he said. "If I had a spot like this near me, I would come here every day. Even though it's cold, this place makes me feel protected and happy. Like the crazy world won't get me."

"Yes! That's how I feel. Protected and happy."

We continued to sit quietly, gazing out into the distance. It reminded me of the times I sat here quietly with Bobby, not saying anything, but feeling so connected to him. It made me sad.

I tried to push the sadness out of my mind. This place was too beautiful to think about being sad. Not on this gorgeously sunny afternoon.

"Do you believe in God?" Mark asked me out of the blue.

I shrugged. "Yes and no," I said. "How's that for an answer?"

Mark nodded. "I get it. I feel the same way sometimes."

"But you're a born-again Christian. All you guys believe in God, don't you?"

Mark turned to me. "There you go. Stereotyping again. Born-again Christians are people, just like everybody else. Strictly speaking, we're Pentecostals," he added. "My family belongs to a denomination called Assemblies of God. That's the world's largest Pentecostal group."

"Oh." All this was new to me.

"And we're not all crazy, backward types," Mark continued, obviously still offended by my comment. "Pentecostals were one of the first religious groups to ordain women."

"I'm sorry," I apologized. "It's easy to stereotype people, isn't it?"

"It's okay. You're not the only one who thinks that about us." He was silent for a bit and then added, "Many people would probably want us to be all the same. But we're not. We're just not."

I could see something was on his mind, so decided to say quiet. Didn't want to upset him again.

I glanced over at Mark after a few minutes. He was frowning

"You okay?" I asked. "You look upset."

Mark shrugged. "A little, I guess."

I waited for him to continue.

"I'm having an argument with my parents," he finally said. "They want to sign me up for a summer camp next year, and I don't want to go."

"You're kidding."

"No, not at all. Summer fellowship camp is a big deal for us. Prayer meetings, Bible study, volunteering, I've gone since I was a kid, though I took a break this past summer, like I told you."

I was looking at him and nodding. "Remember I told you I had the same argument with my folks last summer when they wanted to send me to Lith camp. We're really so similar in so many ways." I smiled. "With religion too. Catholics, especially old-time Lith Catholics, have their own heavy-duty rituals."

"How did you get out of going?"

"Well, I'm not sure," I said, trying to remember. "I had a summer job, so it was a little complicated to take time off. Plus, my parents were busy concentrating on getting their citizenship, so they weren't that focused on me."

"Lucky you. My parents are already citizens. I just don't want to go!" he burst out. "I don't know why, but I still need a break from all that."

I told Mark about the time I refused to go to the Lith dance at Thanksgiving dinner last year. "Can't you put your foot down like I did?"

Mark shook his head. "Not with my parents you don't." He turned to me. "Having a gay brother means all their focus is on me now. Saving me." He turned away again. "Sorry. I didn't mean anything about the gay comment, but it makes it that much worse for me."

"No offense taken." I felt bad seeing how upset Mark was. "I wish I could say something to make you feel better," I added.

"It's okay. It's my cross to bear, as we say in fellowship circles. It's not like I hate everything about the fellowship," he continued. "There are great people there, and we do great things. I like the Saturday morning discussion groups we have, for example. Today's was especially good. About how to succeed in modern life but still keep our faith."

"Yeah. Keeping faith. I think about that too."

"Yes, me too. A lot." Mark still looked agitated. He shook his head. "It's just there's so much fellowship in my life. It's like I can't breathe sometimes. Or have time for other stuff."

"Exactly how I feel!" I said. "I like a lot of Lith things. But I'm trying to make room for other things." I shook my head too. "Maybe it's the immigrant thing, but the big word for my parent is heritage. 'It's your heritage. It's your heritage.' Well, I'm trying to figure out my own heritage."

Mark was nodding. "Yes. Don't you feel like you want to break away from your life sometimes?"

I laughed. "Are you kidding?" I told him about my crazy family and all the arguments at dinner and my brother acting out. "And then the gay thing. Some days, if I knew how to break away, I would. But I just don't know how or to what."

"I guess we're both stuck until we figure things out," Mark said. "At least it's good to know other people are stuck too."

I told him about Mr. Aniso, trying to think of something positive to say. "Maybe you could find someone like that. Someone who knows what you're going through and is happy to listen to you. Being friends with him has helped me a lot."

"Yeah, that would be good. Someone who left the ministry. Wouldn't that be something. Mom and Dad would just about die."

*

I've been thinking a lot about my conversation with Mark. It's amazing. Even though we come from different worlds, we have so much in common. I feel bad for him. He's so upset. It looks like he's wrestling with so many things about this life.

I'm wrestling with many things, too, but I'm not quite that agitated, am I? I feel lucky in one thing. Like I told him, I have Mr. Aniso to talk to. Not that I've seen Mr. Aniso all that often this year, but I know he's always there for me if I need him. He's been like an older brother. An older brother I can trust with my secrets. That's pretty cool.

One thing with Mark though. He's my age. And as cool as it is to have an older brother I can trust with secrets, having a someone my own age I can open up to is great in a different way. He's in the same place as I am as far as so many things are concerned. I don't have try to be adult with him, like I sometimes do with Mr. Aniso. I can just be myself. My crazy, unsure, questioning self. And I know he gets it because he's unsure and questioning too.

We talked about other things on that rock. Like about praying. Mark prays too. When I told him I call God The Big Guy, he looked a little shocked, but then he smiled. So, I think he likes that idea. I told him I have my issues with praying, but I still do it. Can't seem to stop myself. Mark said he understands. Said it's nice to meet someone else who prays. Funny, people don't talk about praying much. Is it one of those super private issues that's not meant to be talked about? Or do people get embarrassed about it, like I do sometimes, since we're not even sure the Big Guy exists?

Mark told me a little more about the fellowship meetings too. Even though he said he wants to break away for a while, he also said he doesn't want to do it totally. He likes the friends he has in the fellowship. And he feels bad about his parents. They're already suffering about his brother. He said they're good people, and he would feel guilty breaking away from them the way his brother has and making them suffer more.

Wow. I realize so much of what he said describes what I feel. Like I said, we come from two different worlds, but in many ways it's the same world. Okay, Big Guy. Is that another one of your lessons? It's an excellent one. I'm happy that your lessons can make me feel good sometimes, not just like I'm punched in the gut. Ha ha. Especially these days when I'm so worried about Bobby.

Mark and I talked on that rock for what seemed like hours. And we felt like we could have talked more. When Mark said he had to go home, he turned to me and gave me a great big hug. I hugged him back. "It's good to have a friend," he said. "A real friend." I told him I felt the same way.

Boy, that rock has seen a lot of dramatic moments of my life. And the best thing is, even though I can come here and be by myself, I never feel alone there.

Chapter Eleven

Holiday Spirit

I finally got to see Bobby today. It was not good.

It's been a month since his injury, and he's still in the hospital. I thought I'm used to hospitals by now, what with going to see Mr. Aniso and Melissa. But this was different.

Bobby was lying in bed at an angle so that the upper part of his body was almost in an upright position. The top of his head was bandaged, and his eyes were closed. A few doctors were crowded around him. There were two chairs at the foot of the bed. Mrs. Marshall was sitting in one of them. She gave me a brief nod and greeting, and then quickly focused her stare back on Bobby.

I sat down in the other chair. One of the doctors was shining a light into Bobby's eyes with some sort of instrument. "Good," he was saying. "Very good, Bobby."

He turned to the other two doctors leaning over Bobby. "He's doing well. Very well."

The doctors started talking among themselves. The doctors were throwing around words like "post-concussion syndrome," "cranial pressure," "optic nerve damage," and "cognitive impairment." They sounded pretty scary. Luckily, intermixed with those words were more positive-sounding ones. "Progress." "So much better than before." "The shunt did the trick." "We made the right decision." "Additional drug therapy for recovery."

The doctors finished examining Bobby and started to leave. The doctor who had been shining the light into Bobby's eyes turned to Mrs. Marshall.

"Good news, Mrs. Marshall," the doctor said. "Bobby is doing better. We think we've saved the optic nerve."

"You're sure?" Mrs. Marshall asked.

"As sure as we can be in these cases," the doctor said. "There may be some other cognitive damage. But Bobby is strong. With rehab, he should improve. Maybe get back to his old self."

"Maybe?"

The doctor looked apologetic. "I wish I could say definitely. But we just don't know so many things yet. It's too early in Bobby's recovery." The doctor touched her gently on the shoulder. "Mrs. Marshall, Bobby is strong. It will take a while, but he is now definitely on the road to recovery. Don't give up hope."

"I won't. I can't,' she replied. With that Mrs. Marshall burst into tears. She took out a Kleenex and blew her nose, apologizing to me. Then she got up and walked over to the bed.

"Oh, Bobby. Oh, Bobby. You'll be all right." Mrs. Marshall gently caressed his cheek. "Did you hear the doctors? You'll be all right. You'll be all right."

Bobby opened his eyes, smiled briefly, and then closed them again.

"And you have a visitor," she said. "Are you up for a visitor?"

Bobby opened his eyes and turned to me slowly.

"RV."

"Bobby."

Bobby smiled weakly again. "Good to see you, RV," he mumbled, before closing his eyes again.

"I'm going downstairs to the cafeteria for a cup of coffee. I'll be back in a few minutes," Mrs. Marshall said to me. When she was halfway out of the room, she turned back to me. "Remember what the doctor said. Bobby is strong. We have to have hope." Was she reminding me? Herself? Or both of us?

I nodded. She left and I stayed rooted in the chair, not sure what to say or do. All I could think about were Mrs. Marshall's words, clattering around in my brain.

Bobby opened his eyes and kept staring at me. He smiled again. "Sorry, RV. This isn't a football game for you to cheer me on," he finally said.

"It's—it's okay," was about the only way I could respond. "I'm just glad to see you."

"I'm glad to see you too."

Bobby turned his head back away from me and closed his eyes once more, but he continued talking. "I'm tired. So tired. Tests. Doctors. More tests. I think I had an operation."

"Oh?"

"I don't want more operations. I want to go home."

"I think you'll be able to. Did you hear what the doctor said to your mom?"

"No."

"He said now you're on the road to recovery." I didn't add the stuff about other possible—what was the word?—cognitive damage.

Hearing myself say those words aloud scared me. Did it mean that before the doctors weren't sure Bobby would recover? Recover from what? Losing his eyesight?

I had to repeat what I had just said, maybe to convince myself too. "Did you hear me, Bobby? You're on the road to recovery."

Bobby nodded slightly, his eyes still closed, but he didn't say anything. "Good. I better be."

I told myself it was time to go. Bobby needed to rest. Luckily, Mrs. Marshall reappeared in the doorway, so I felt comfortable leaving.

I got up from the chair. Bobby's arm was lying on top of the blanket, so I went up and squeezed his hand. "'Bye, Bobby," I said, "I'll see you soon."

Bobby gave me a little squeeze back. Was it just my wish or did he really mumble, "See you soon, RV."

I said goodbye to Mrs. Marshall and left for home.

*

I cried as I went to bed last night. Just lay there in bed, tears going down my cheeks like a child.

I was crying for Bobby, and for myself too. I had been hoping to go there to cheer him up, the way I had cheered up Mr. Aniso. But the visit didn't go that way, did it? Bobby was in worse shape than Mr. Aniso when I saw him in the hospital that first time. All those doctors. Those frightening-sounding terms. His head bandaged. I know concussions aren't great. But this sounds worse. How bad is Bobby's injury? What does additional cognitive damage mean?

They did promise Mrs. Marshall he would recover. Didn't they? I tried not think about the word maybe. It was too frightening. Instead, I kept trying to remember the positive words they used and repeated them to myself over and over. I needed to. Because the way Bobby was just lying there, practically comatose, didn't look very promising.

*

So much for the holiday spirit. Instead of enjoying the red Santa Clauses, colored lights, and Christmas trees, I keep thinking about Bobby. Who wants to spend Christmas in the hospital? I'm wondering when the doctors will let Bobby go home. I think I've had enough hospital visits to last me a long time.

Mom and Dad keep trying to get me into the Christmas spirit. The demonstrations about the merger of the churches have stopped for the holidays. That gives Mom and Dad time for other things. Dad is doing his donations-for-Lithuania's-orphans thing in a big way. And guess who's helping him as he drives around, collecting packages, wrapping and addressing the packages, going to the post office, making calls and soliciting donations. I never thought I'd say this, but I'm glad to be doing it. Keeping me so busy is taking my mind off Bobby.

Mom has been working extra hours at Neiman Marcus for the holidays, but she still has time to bake cakes for some parties they go to. At least no more Christmas pageants for Lith School. Mom's too busy this year and bowed out. I heard this year the kids have to enact Christmas Eve in the manger, when the animals talk, according to the Liths. Cute tradition, so long as Ray or I don't have to participate, playing a goat or a sheep, as we did in the old days. *Moo moo. Baa baa.*

Thank you, Big Guy, sincerely for those small favors. You might not answer the big requests, at least not right away, but I appreciate you keeping us away from those pageants. The benefits of getting older!

I was about to thank the Big Guy for keeping us away from those Christmas pageants, but then I stopped myself. Maybe the Big Guy has nothing to do with it in this case. Maybe it's just the benefits of getting older, LOL.

And what about my PSAT scores? We got them back. I was hoping for at least a 700 score for Reading and Writing and I did—720 out of a possible 760. Go, RV! I was worried about Math, but I got 570. Passable, right? So, my total was 1290 out of 1520.It means I just made the ninetieth percentile! Okay, okay. I have to admit it. I did sneak in a little thanks to the Big Guy. Whether He had anything to do with my scores or not, I feel good about them.

I tried to explain the complicated scoring system to Mom and Dad, because there are all these other scores they give you, like a scaled score and a raw score and a subscore. Makes your head hurt. The College Board people just want to drive kids and parents crazy, as if we don't have enough pressure already. I kept emphasizing the ninetieth percentile to Mom and Dad, better than ninety percent of the other kids who took the test, so they were happy.

"Labai gerai, Arvydai."

"Mokykis! Mokykis!"

"Nauduok savo smegenis!"

"Didžiuojames tavim!"

"Very good, RV."

"Study. Study!"

"Use that brain of yours!"

"We're so proud of you!"

So, what would they say if I fell in the fiftieth percentile? Or lower? Ray, of course, gave me a dirty look as they were praising me, because with his Bs and Cs he expects to be around that percentile. If he's lucky.

I don't want to brag, but I do feel good about doing well. I don't think I'll qualify for a National Merit Scholarship like Jonas, my genius Super Lith cousin, but in being in the ninetieth percentile, I can hold my own with Mrs. S-head. If she says anything condescending the next time we get together, I'll just say I'm happy with that score and leave it at that. "After all, Mrs. S-head. I'm not Jonas. Nor do I ever want to be." Oh, wouldn't it be great to say that someday!

*

We went to Midnight Mass tonight. Mom still insists we go, though at least we don't have to drive all the way to South Boston any longer for the Lith mass. Mom's happy enough with an English mass, so we go here in West Roxbury.

"After all, God knows English," as Ray always says.

"Yeah. He must know about seven hundred languages," I added this year, as we were driving to church.

Mom and Dad didn't say anything to my little joke. I started wondering how many languages there really were in the world and promised myself I would Google that when we got home.

In church, my mind was on serious things. I prayed. And I didn't feel bad about it. I prayed harder than I have in a long time. I asked that God would help Bobby recover quickly. That's all the Christmas present I would need. Then I tried to focus on the other method of praying for once, listening instead of talking. Really tried. Did I hear anything? I found myself thinking about poor Bobby again, lying there bandaged up in the hospital bed. But then I thought about my good health and was thankful for it.

The priest's sermon was about family and a reminder that those of us who have families should be happy and think of all those people who don't have one.

I glanced over at my family as he was talking. Dad was sitting there, his hands on his lap, and his eyes closed. I wondered what he was thinking. Was he happy for his family here? What about the family he left behind in the Old Country? Hopefully, he didn't want to go back. He still had a job, I reminded myself. That was another reason to stay here.

Mom was sitting there praying, kneeling, her face in her cupped hands. She looked so devout. What was she praying about? Me? Ray? Happy that Ray wasn't acting out so much this year? Happy that I was turning out okay? What would she pray for if she knew what else was going on inside me?

And what about Ray? He sat on the bench quietly, but he did sneak his cell phone out a few times. Was Roberta sending him texts? He was certainly smitten with her. Was that why he was behaving so differently this year? Love is amazing, isn't it?

And me? Where was I in this family? The priest said we should count our blessings. Priests often say sentimental things. But thinking about Bobby made me realize that, yeah, there are a few good things in my life. I don't see Carole much anymore, but I did make a new friend of Mark. And I did get those good PSAT scores. And Mr. Aniso is still around, even though I haven't seen him as much this term as before. And my family, well, I'm sure they'll still drive me crazy next year, but I'll be able to forgive them, right? As long as Bobby recovers, I'll be able to forgive just about anything.

So was all that me listening to the Big Guy? Who knows? I did feel better, though, for the first time in a while at church. The pretty red flowers and the lights that decorate the church this time of year cheered me up too.

PS: I googled language in the world when we got home. Wow! There are over six thousand spoken languages! I'll have to cut The Big Guy some more slack. If He doesn't answer me, I'll have to remember he's processing all those languages. Coming at Him, twenty-four seven. If He has ears, they must hurt, ha ha!

Chapter Twelve

Happy New Year?

Well, if the New Year is supposed to bring good news, I'm still waiting. Carole was not in the best shape either when she called me.

"Can we meet at Joe's? I need to talk." She sounded far from her old, cheerful self.

"Joe's is closed."

"What?"

I told her the whole sad story. Even went there the day before they closed to ask Joe if he had any news. He shook his head and looked downbeat. Something didn't work out. But he still took my phone number, saying he was working on other possibilities. He told me he'd text me as soon as there was something to report.

"Yes," I told him. "Please. Please do."

"Wow. What a terrible start to the New Year," Carole said, sniffling.

I asked her if she wanted me to come over to her house.

"No," she said. "I've been in the house too long. Spent Christmas week cooped up here. I need to get out."

No wonder I hadn't seen or heard from her during Christmas. I thought she was busy with her French visitor François, so I didn't want to bother her. But maybe she was sick.

I asked her if she wanted to come over to my house, but she said she wasn't sick and wanted to be outside. So, we agreed to go to the woods, to "our" place. "Our" place, ha. I didn't want to tell her that our place had become my place with Bobby, and now my place with Mark. Funny. Maybe it's okay to keep it "our place" with whoever I take there. No need to tell them it's somebody else's place too.

Am I being Machiavellian? I learned about Machiavelli in history class before the holiday break. He sounds like a scary dude. But a smart dude too. Scary and cynical, telling people how to get what you want in life. Even doing bad things to get power. His book was *The Prince*, but I don't know if he was a prince. I wonder how he knew so much about power then. I guess you don't have to be a prince to know about power. Look at Latin School. A lot of power is used and abused here. I could write a book about it. Call it *The Teacher*. Talk about Mr. Aniso. The other teachers. The students. Duffy and Doyle. McGrath. Flaberty. Other bullies in gym class. Maybe I should call it *High School Teachers: A Mixed Bag*.

I was still coming up with titles for my book about power when Carole and I got to our rock in the woods and sat down. It was cold, and I remembered the time she and I sat there when it started snowing.

"Even though there's no snow, this place still looks magical, doesn't it?" I said, looking out into the distance. "The power of nature. Now that's real power."

Carole gave me a questioning look.

"We've been studying about Machiavelli in history class. Talk about power."

She didn't seem very interested, looking far away somewhere.

"I've been thinking about power," I said. I hugged her. "C'mon, what's the matter? Will you tell me now?"

Carole was still quiet, staring down at the ground. Then, after a little more coaxing from me, it all came out. François didn't come to visit for the holidays. He told her his parents had changed their plans, and she hasn't heard from him since.

"Well, that's the French for you," I said. "Easy kiss, easy go."

Carole gave me a dirty look. So much for me and my lame jokes.

"I'm just trying to make you laugh." I gave her another hug.

She wrapped her coat more tightly around herself and snuggled into me. "I know, I know," she said. "But you need to come up with something better."

"I'll try."

"The thing is, I thought François really liked me. He actually told me he loved me once."

"Maybe what they consider love is different in France," I said before I could stop myself.

Luckily, Carole ignored my comment and continued talking. "I mean, why did he write me those e-mails and WhatsApps if he didn't mean it?"

"Maybe he meant it at the time."

"And now he's changed so quickly?" Carole gave me a sharp look. "I haven't heard from him since that message before Christmas. Is that the French way too?"

I didn't know what to say, not wanting to upset her more.

"There's something else." Carole looked out into the distance again. "Tim and I had a fight. A bad fight yesterday."

"About what?"

"About the computer business. I got the feeling he wanted to push me out totally and have snot-nosed Loretta take my place. He doesn't want any more consulting from me." She shook her head angrily. "After all the work you and I did to get things started! He thinks he can just waltz in and take over!"

"I knew he was bad news! That's what we get for trusting him."

"I know. You were right to have your doubts."

"I actually wondered if you and he were going out," I admitted. "It seemed like it for a while. Like when I saw you two at the Halloween party."

"Yeah, we were getting close," Carole said. "To tell you the truth, I was wondering the same thing. I thought Tim liked me, but I didn't let it go anywhere because of François." She paused and shook her head. "And now look what happened. I got screwed. Ha ha." She nudged me. "My turn to make a lame joke." She picked up a pebble that was there on the rock beside her and flung it out into the grass. "Relationships. They're crazy. Who can figure them out?"

More than anything at that moment I wanted to tell her more about my friendship with Bobby. I even started to say something about friendships and then stopped myself. Why is my promise to him so strong that I can't say anything about us? To anyone? I saw how mad he was when I said something to Mr. Aniso. But that was then. Now is different, isn't it? After visiting him in the hospital, I almost feel like Bobby's not Bobby anymore. What a terrible thought.

Carole and I talked some more about friendships and relationships, and how they could make you nuts. Then we got cold. I offered her to come to my house to warm up and for some hot chocolate. But she said no. She wanted to go home and think about how she wanted to respond to Tim.

Business, we agreed, could be as crazy as relationships.

*

One good thing is happening. Mr. Felucci, our stern math teacher, was so impressed with our climate change ideas at the Halloween party, he started a new project this term for the entire school. It's called "It Starts at Home," and is all about what you can do at home to combat climate change. Anyone who wants to be involved in the project can come to the periodic meetings, where they can share new ideas and research, discuss the progress they've made in becoming more carbon neutral at home, and compare notes on what they can do to help bring their parents on board to make changes. There might even be a prize at the end of the school year. I think it's a good idea. Mark and I decided we'd look in on some of the meetings if we have time and see what information we could pick up.

Funny how people can change personalities. Blubber-faced Mr. Felucci might not be as pretty as Miss Sánchez, but when he talks about climate change, he becomes so likable. Totally different than he is in class with his theorems and postulates. He smiles and makes jokes. Comes across as a funny, nice guy. Reminds me of Ed at the gas station last summer—most of the time.

Maybe the best thing is that Ray is also into the spirit of combating climate change. He says Roberta and her entire family are big into it, so that's why he's big on it. Though I'd like to believe that my calling attention to it at home has influenced him too. Whatever the reason, it's great. He's much more energetic about it than I am.

He goes around shutting off lights the minute Mom and Dad leave a room. And he's been after Dad to switch to energy-efficient light bulbs. The other day, when Mom complained about supermarkets not offering plastic bags anymore, he read her the riot act. He told her that banning them was a good thing and that she better not bring another plastic bag into the house.

I know we drive Mom and Dad a little crazy, but it's for a good cause, so I don't care. I've been talking to them about bigger issues. The other day at dinner, I brought down my laptop and tried to show them a link to a website that measures your carbon footprint.

"It's a carbon calculator," I said to them when they looked at me puzzled. "Just like the costume I had at the Halloween party, but this is the real thing."

Mom pretended to be interested for a few seconds, but Dad just grumbled and went back to eating.

"No, no, it's good!" I insisted. "Look." I clicked on the link and moved the laptop so they could better see the screen. "Look, here," I repeated. "You fill out these blanks and tally everything up. Did you know all these things affect our carbon footprint?" I started to list them. "The things in our house. The make of our car. The gas we buy. The fuel we use. The planes, buses, and trains we take. The computers we use."

Mom and Dad were still more focused on eating than looking at the screen. But I persevered. "All these things add up. Did you know that the average carbon footprint for the United States is over sixteen metric tons? In Europe it's six metric tons. But it should be no more than two metric tons."

Ray spoke up too. "Dad, do you know about AFUE?"

Dad told him he wouldn't respond if he spoke English.

Ray rolled his eyes but switched to the Mother Tongue. "*Ar žinai apie* AFUE?"

Of course, Dad didn't know.

"It's the Annual Fuel Utilization Efficiency rating." Ray switched back to English. He told Dad he learned that gas furnaces have a higher rating than oil furnaces. Since we have oil heat in our house, he told Dad he should consider changing our furnace.

Dad, of course, couldn't let that go. He told Ray he would consider doing it if Ray gave him five thousand dollars for a new heating system.

Ray switched his argument. He said we shouldn't be using fossil fuels anyway. That we should consider alternative sources of energy like solar panels, wood stoves, and geothermal energy.

That pleased Dad. He told Ray a wood stove was a great idea. He told Ray he'd give him the axe he had in his tool shed and he would go out with Ray every morning before school to chop down some trees just like his grandfather did back in the Old Country. I'm glad he didn't add how many miles his grandfather walked through the snow.

"*Nekalbėk niekų,*" Mom said to Dad. "Don't talk nonsense." She went back to eating, but I didn't want to let her off the hook either.

"*Taip,*" I said, renewing my argument and wanting to defend Ray. "*Nereikia kirsti medžių, bet galim daryti kitus dalykus.*" "We don't have to chop down trees, but we can do other things."

I reminded them the school initiative was called It Starts at Home. Mom has been complaining about our old car lately. I told them if they do buy a new car, they should consider a hybrid.

"Or an electric car," Ray suggested.

That turned the discussion into one about money again. And so it goes, round and round at our house. If nothing else, though, maybe Ray and I are raising a bit of awareness. It's so good to be doing something Ray and I agree on. Maybe it's the start of a new relationship between us. That would be something. Starting with a bad relationship and making it better.

Not that I expect miracles. Hear that, Big Guy? Ha ha. Ray still doesn't talk about much else to me except climate change. But it's a start, isn't it? And if there's one thing I've learned in my fifteen years on this planet it's that you can't expect miracles very often. That's why they're called miracles.

Okay, okay. I have my doubts about miracles. But what about minimiracles? I think I believe in those. There are more of them than you think. They just start small. Who would have thought a year ago that I'd be friends, good friends, with Mr. Aniso, my Latin teacher? Or that I'd be doing okay at Latin School? Or that I'd be friends with a football player, as crazy as that friendship has been? Or even crazier, that the football player said he likes me, even if that might not be true anymore?

*

Another nice thing I've discovered about Mark. He enjoys going to movies, just like Carole and I do. I'd like to introduce him to Carole. Mark seems sad so often, I think being with Carole might cheer him up. That is, providing Carole gets over François. She used to be so much fun. Now she's still in that miserable funk. Man, relationships can really screw you up. Don't I know it!

Anyway, I was trying to think of a movie that all three of us could go to, a cheerful movie, when Mark texted me. He asked me if I wanted to go to a movie called *Summer of Love on the Dunes*. It's about four high school friends, two guys and two girls, who spend their summer on Cape Cod. They find love, lose it, and then find it and lose it again. It's R-rated. Mark said he heard other people snuck into the movie easily, so we should try too.

"We have things to learn about love," Mark said, telling me about the movie. "And besides, it's supposed to have nice scenery."

The movie sounded a little dorky to me, even if it was R-rated. But I said I'd go and asked if I could tell Carole about it too. Seemed perfect for her. Mark said sure. But no matter how much I cajoled (good word—something my parents do to me all the time), Carole said she wasn't interested in love right now. Okay, Carole needs more time to feel sorry for herself. I guess all of us get like that at times. I told myself to cut her some slack, but not leave her alone for too long. The tricky part of being friends, I suppose.

So, it would be just Mark and me. That was okay. I haven't seen Mark since before the holidays. It turns out his family has almost as many Christmas rituals as we do. They go to services, they distribute gifts to kids, they do outreach to families in need, they see relatives.

"Yeah, it's been a busy time," Mark said when we met for the movie. "I'm almost glad to be back at school."

"Yeah, I know what you mean," I agreed. "Does that mean we're not kids anymore? Preferring to be back at school, rather than on vacation?"

Mark shrugged. "Maybe. But I don't really feel like an adult either."

I agreed with that too. "Yeah. So, what do we call ourselves? The Between Generation? Maybe we'll feel more like adults after we see this movie," I added, hopefully.

"Yeah. Getting into an R movie means you're an adult."

"It does?" I laughed.

"Sure. R movies do have pretty good love scenes. Keep your fingers crossed. Maybe we'll get lucky, and this one will have really hot ones."

I crossed my two fingers. "Okay. My fingers are crossed right now. Let's see if we get lucky."

As soon as we started watching the movie, I understood why Mark picked it. One of the two girls, Mary, the one a guy named Matt liked, wasn't a girl at all. She was an older woman. Maybe twenty-five or even thirty. She was married, and her husband went off somewhere because they weren't getting along. She was beautiful too. For a second, as she was coming down the beach in her red bikini, I thought it was Miss Sánchez. The actress looked just like her.

I nudged Mark. "So, this is why we came," I joked. "I feel like I'm in Spanish class."

I could tell Mark was mesmerized, even in the dark. "Yeah," he whispered, not looking away from the screen. "Yeah."

The movie was predictable, at least in the beginning. But if you liked sexy babes in bikinis, you weren't bored.

But then the movie focused more on the other couple, Frank and Phoebe. Phoebe was pretty, and Frank was muscular and sensitive, the kind of man that doesn't exist in real life, except for Bobby. The movie showed them sitting on the dune, talking, falling more and more in love. Then they began to make out. Now I was getting mesmerized. I looked at both of them, but, of course, the truth is I spent more time looking at Frank. Why can't I just accept it once and for all? The guy was sexier, and I wanted the scene to go on for a long time.

Then the movie took a really interesting turn. Matt and Frank got together on the beach at sunset. They were still in their swim trunks having just come in from an evening swim. They started to compare notes on how well they were doing with their attempts to score with Mary and Phoebe. The more they talked the more romantically they looked at one another. And then they started kissing and rolling around in the sand.

I've never been so excited in my life. And embarrassed too. I got a huge erection. I stared straight ahead at the screen, afraid to look at Mark. Not that we hadn't talked about my being gay, but this was different. An erection is private. One of the most private things there is a about a guy.

And it was a reminder, too, as if I needed another one. A reminder from my body that being gay was part of me and I couldn't run away from it. Though I've tried to push it out of my mind umpteen times.

"I didn't know there was a gay theme in this movie," I said to Mark as we were leaving.

Mark looked kind of sheepish. "I knew there would be a little bit, but I didn't realize it would be such a big part of the plot."

"So, at the end of the movie, you know that Mary seduces Matt. And that Matt and Frank make out. But do they all end up with someone past the summer? Or were these just temporary summer flings?"

"I'm not sure. I guess we have to figure it out for ourselves."

We went for a burger before heading home. "What are you thinking about?" I asked Mark, who was looking even more lost in thought than usual. Poor guy. Mark seems to have even more thoughts rattling around in this brain than I do. Another reason I like him, I suppose.

"What are you thinking about?" I asked again when Mark didn't answer me. He really seemed to be in another world.

"Oh, sorry. I'm still thinking about the movie," he finally said.

"You mean the Miss Sánchez lookalike?" I teased. "I can see why."

"Yeah." But I could see Mark's mind was still somewhere else.

"Did the gay part bother you?" I asked him.

"No. No," he said quickly. But I saw he was blushing. "Did you like it?"

"I guess so." I tried to put on that nonchalant look. "Though I have nothing to compare it to."

Mark thought for a second and then asked, "Is that what two guys do?"

"I don't know," I answered. "I've never done anything like that." It wasn't a lie, was it? Bobby and I did kiss, but never like that. And never in a romantic place like a beach at sunset.

Mark asked me a few more questions about how guys "did it." Most of the time, I had to shake my head and say I had no idea. I was starting to feel like I was being grilled about something I had no experience of. Why did Mark assume I knew so much about gay life when I knew so little about it? It's not like you press a button and you automatically know about being gay. And I'm not sure I'm totally gay either. I could go for making out with Miss Sánchez or Mary in the red bikini.

I was glad when it was time to go home. I wasn't sure whether it was the movie or Mark's questions or a combination of both, but I was exhausted. I just wanted to go home and rest.

*

The movie really affected me. Going to bed, I kept picturing Matt and Frank making out on the beach. It made me think how much I would like to do that with Bobby. But those thoughts were quickly replaced by sadness. The chances of that happening were now so far away if not nonexistent. Bobby had to recover first. I almost wished I hadn't gone to the hospital to see him. It wasn't Bobby who was there in that hospital bed. It was someone weak and tired with bandages around his head. A shell of the Bobby I knew. It nearly made me cry again.

I had a dream about the movie too. I was sitting there on the beach at sunset. But it wasn't with Bobby. It was with Mark. We were talking about something, and Mark started asking me about being gay. He asked a lot of questions, just like he did in real life. Questions I didn't know the answers to. He kept asking them, though, getting more and more angry that I didn't know how to respond. Then Miss Sánchez came by in a red bikini. She took both of us by the hand and said, "I know the answers." She led us away, down the dune, and into the ocean. But the water was cold, and I woke up.

Man, it's the middle of the night, but I just had to write down this dream. I really have to study more about Sigmund Freud. He wrote about sex and dreams and the unconscious. I wish he were around so I could talk to him. What is going on with my unconscious? Do dreams really say anything? Too bad old Sigmund is long gone. I suppose Mr. Aniso is a good second choice to talk to. But does he know anything about dreams?

Aha! I just ordered *The Interpretation of Dreams* from Amazon. If Mom and Dad ask me about it, I can tell them it's for a class. Don't need to tell them it's about me. I hope I find some answers there. The Big Guy isn't helping. Not with my dreams anyway. I suppose it's not His specialty. But it's Sigmund's. And the book is only a little over a hundred pages. So, figuring out dreams can't be that complicated, can it?

Chapter Thirteen

Where Does the Hate Come From?

Great news! I went by Joe's today and saw a new sign in the window. It started with the words WE'VE MOVED, and it gave the new address. The new address was only a few blocks away, so I rushed over there.

There were no other customers in the place. But Joe was there, fiddling with something near the cash register.

"RV! Welcome!" he said, seeing me.

"Hey, Joe! This is your new place?"

"I told you I was working on something." Joe looked pleased with himself. "I wanted to tell you, RV, but I didn't want to jinx anything." He smiled as he watched me looking around. "So, you approve of the place? The opinion of my customers matters." He winked at me. "Especially yours."

This Joe's was a little smaller than the other place, but there still were a few booths to relax in and a few small tables too. Even a small counter by a large side window where customers could sit on stools and look outside.

"This was already a pizza joint," Joe said. "So, it came ready-made." He went over to the ovens and patted the side. "Most important thing, the ovens. Brick ovens. The best. I didn't have to spend extra."

I'd never seen Joe so happy. He came out from behind the counter and continued talking, looking around himself. "It's a good place, yes? It needs a little work, but I'll spruce it up to make it feel like home. You approve? Yes, RV?"

"I approve. I approve," I told him, laughing.

But Joe wasn't finished. "And guess what?"

"What?"

"I own it. Yes! No more rent. The previous owner was a simple *paisan*, like me." Joe cupped his fingers together and made a motion with his hand the way Italians are supposed to. "He's a good man, the previous owner. And he quoted me a good price." He turned to me and put his hands on my shoulders. "RV, things turn out for the best!" he said, giving my shoulders a little shake. "We need to celebrate." He turned around and went back behind the counter. "You can stay for a slice, yes? It will be on the house. For my longtime customer in my new pizzeria!"

"Sure." Joe's great mood was making me feel good too. "We'll see if you've still got the magic pizza touch," I teased.

"Dare you doubt me, my young friend?" Joe teased back. "Just you wait and see. I told you. Things work out for the best."

*

I got another piece of good news after coming home from Joe's. Mr. Marshall called me to say Bobby was home from the hospital and resting comfortably. I asked him if I could come over, thinking I could surprise him with something from Joe's, but Mr. Marshall asked me to wait a few days.

"Bobby is still adjusting to being home," he explained. "Besides, he's still very tired and sleeping a lot," he added a little more ominously. "He needs a lot of rest."

"Okay. Let me know when Bobby's up for a visit."

Mr. Marshall told me he definitely would, that I was first on the list for visitors.

It was hard to concentrate on school and daily life while I was waiting for that phone call. Especially when a few days turned into a week, then two. But finally, I heard from Mr. Marshall that Bobby would be happy to see me.

I was happy, too, to get that phone call, even though I was a little surprised it was Mr. Marshall who called and not Bobby himself. What was that all about?

Putting the thought out of my mind, I went over to Joe's and ordered a whole pizza with the best vegetables Joe could put on them.

"You got it," Joe said, preparing the pizza. "With all these vegetables, there will be enough vitamins here to get Bobby back on his feet in no time."

"Thanks. But give me a few slices of pepperoni," I said, laughing. "I don't need any vegetables on my pizza. I bet Bobby's parents prefer pepperoni too."

Joe teased me some more and then handed me everything packed up nicely once the pizza was ready.

"Give my best to Bobby," he said. "Tell him I'm waiting for his visit so I can give him his free slice."

"Will do," I promised. "It won't take too long if I have anything to do with it."

*

I took a few deep breaths when I rang the doorbell to Bobby's house. I hoped it would be very different from the hospital visit. Those images of Bobby lying there with his head bandaged up kept popping up in my mind too frequently.

Bobby's father answered the door.

"Hi, RV," he said. "Good to see you."

"Good to see you, too, Mr. Marshall," I said awkwardly.

He led me inside. "How have you been?" he asked. I could see he tried to smile, but the smile was strained. No surprise with everything they were going through.

"I've been fine," I told Mr. Marshall. I held out the pizza. "This is for all of us. The healthy stuff for Bobby, and a couple of pepperoni slices for the rest of us."

Mr. Marshall took the pizza and laughed, thanking me for not sticking to vegetables only.

At that point Mrs. Marshall came out of the kitchen. She seemed cheerful enough. She hugged me and thanked me for the pizza when Mr. Marshall told her what I had brought.

Mr. Marshall took the pizza to the kitchen and Mrs. Marshall led me to Bobby. "Come. Bobby is in the study. It's now his bedroom." She turned back to me as I followed her to the study, which was on the first floor. "And I'm sorry I may have to limit your visit," she told me. "We'll see how it goes. Bobby's still rather weak and gets tired easily. So, I don't want to overdo it."

"Okay, I understand," I said.

I put on a happy face as Mrs. Marshall opened the door to the study and told Bobby his best friend was here.

Well, that made my happy face genuine. So, Bobby still considered me a best friend.

Bobby was lying on a sofa. The TV was on, with the volume turned very low. But Bobby wasn't really watching it, lying still, his eyes closed. His head wasn't bandaged up the way it had been in the hospital, though there was still something covering up one side.

"Hi, Bobby," I said, as cheerfully as I could.

He turned his head slightly and opened his eyes. "Hi," he said.

"Hi, Bobby."

His mother asked if he needed anything, but Bobby shook his head. She also asked me if I wanted anything to eat or drink. I shook my head too. She moved the blanket up to cover more of Bobby's chest, told us to have a nice chat, and then left the room.

"How are you?" I asked, looking down at Bobby.

"Good to see you, RV," Bobby said softly, ignoring my question. "Sit down."

I sat in the chair off to side by the sofa. Bobby turned toward the TV. A cartoon was showing.

"Don't mind the TV," he said. "Cartoons. That's the only thing I can concentrate on these days. Part of my rehab." He turned away and closed his eyes again.

"I—I brought you guys some pizza from Joe's," I said. "The new Joe's."

"The new Joe's?"

"Oh, I guess you missed all that." I told him about Joe's closing and finding a new place. "It's very nice. Joe made me promise I'd bring you there soon for a free slice."

Bobby nodded. "That's nice," he said without too much enthusiasm. He opened his eyes again and turned to me. "Sorry. I'm not being a good host. I'm still a little tired."

I noticed all the prescription pill bottles on a side table in the corner of the room. A few other things were moved down here from his bedroom. But nothing to do with football. His posters and trophies must have stayed upstairs.

Bobby raised his head a bit and pointed to the side with the bandage. "And my head is still not totally right. So sorry I can't entertain you too well."

"I didn't expect you to entertain me," I answered. "I just wanted to say hi and see how you were doing."

"I'll live. I think." Bobby put his head back on the pillow and closed his eyes again. Was that a little laugh from him I heard? Or just a grunt?

"Of course, you'll live. People recover from concussions all the time."

Bobby was quiet for a second. "This was a serious concussion. They were afraid I had Second Impact Syndrome."

"What's that?"

"That's when you have a second concussion after you've already had one, and the first one hasn't totally healed." Bobby told me the first time he had been injured he ignored the headaches he was getting after the game. "Who doesn't get headaches? So, I didn't say anything at the time. Besides, I wanted to get back on the field." He opened his eyes again and turned to me. "Apparently, though, my brain did get whacked a little that first time.

And then on Thanksgiving Day, *wham*! My brain really got it."

He was silent for a while, keeping his eyes open and staring straight ahead. It was hard to watch him like that, and I was glad he started talking again, no matter how slowly and quietly.

"They were afraid my brain was starting to swell," he continued. He turned to me again and actually smiled, trying to make a joke. "I thought my brain getting bigger is a good thing. But it's not." He turned back away. He pointed to the bandage on the side of his head. "They had to do some kind of operation. Put a tube in there to drain fluid. A shunt they call it. Otherwise they were afraid I was going to die."

"Wow," was all I could manage to say.

"Maybe that would have been better," he said.

"Don't talk like that!" I told him.

Bobby ignored me. He closed his eyes again and lay still for a long time. I was about to ask him if I should go, when he opened his eyes, raised himself on one elbow, and asked me to hand him a glass of water that was on that side table with all the pill bottles. I got it for him, he took a few sips, and then lay back down again.

"Look at me now," he finally said, giving me a disgusted look. "I'm an invalid. I'm still tired. I still have headaches. And I still can't do any serious brain work." He let out that half laugh half grunt again. "They say I have some cognitive impairment. A fancy word, which means I can barely watch cartoons! Isn't that a joke? A great, big fucking joke!"

I kept trying to think of something to say to comfort him, but everything seemed so lame.

"I heard the doctors at the hospital," I finally blurted out. "They think you'll be okay. You just have to give it time."

"Oh, yeah. They think!" he practically spat the words out. "They don't know! We have to give it time. Give it time. Fucking time!" Bobby's anger must have given him a little energy because he half sat up on the sofa and leaned toward me. "You know the best part, RV?"

"The best part?"

"Yes. The best part is that I've been forbidden to play all sports for the rest of the school year." He paused and then added, "Or maybe for the rest of my life."

I didn't know what to say.

"Yeah. For. The. Rest. Of. My. Life."

He lay back down on the sofa, closed his eyes, and was silent. I wondered if he was thinking about what he had just said or wanted me to let the words sink in.

I didn't. I couldn't, and I had an idea, wanting to get him to stop thinking about his injury. "Hey, maybe I can read to you," I said. "I can get some books out of the library and read them out loud to you. That will help you, no?"

"What? Read to the invalid? No, thank you!"

"I'm sorry. I didn't mean to get you upset. I—"

"Upset? I'm more than upset. Do you realize what kind of shape I'm in, RV? I nearly died!" He opened his eyes and sat up again with renewed energy.

"I know. I was just trying to help."

"That's nice. But it's not going to help with these headaches or get me off these pills that make me feel like I'm swimming under water." Bobby gestured to the table in the corner of the room. I had to admit I've never seen so many little plastic prescription bottles in one place before.

"Look, Bobby, I know what you're going through. I—"

"Oh, do you?" Bobby interrupted me again. "You have no idea—"

Why was he angry at me?

"But give me some points for trying, okay?" Now I was getting angry, despite myself. "You're not being fair."

"Fair?" Bobby actually laughed. "Who said life is fair?"

The image of Mr. Aniso lying in the hospital bed came to me. "Yeah, it's not fair. It sucks even. But we've got to try."

Bobby laughed again. "Look who's lecturing me." He pushed himself a little higher on the sofa and turned to me, his face not far from mine. His eyes were darker than I'd ever seen them and full of anger. "Do you know how many hours I've sacrificed? Not just on the field. But from my life! Do you have any idea what it takes for a Black guy to be taken seriously?"

"Hey!" I couldn't stop my own anger either. "I know about sacrifices, too, Bobby. Plenty of them!"

"Not like what I'm talking about, white boy!"

"Don't call me names! I can call you plenty of names!"

"I bet you could. Which ones? *Which ones*!"

"Fuck you! *Fuck you*!"

"I think you better leave. Get out of here!"

Bobby started coughing and collapsed back down on the sofa. I jumped up and ran out of the room.

No words came out of my mouth, but plenty of them were stuck in my throat. And better that they stayed there because who knows what would have come out?

*

I was shaking when I left Bobby's house, barely able to say goodbye to his parents and ignoring their offers of having some pizza. What had just happened? I went there with good intentions, but, in the end, Bobby and I said these horrible things to one another.

I went home, slammed the door shut to my room, and threw myself on my bed. I lay there, pretty much in a catatonic state all afternoon. I couldn't even cry. After a while, everyone started asking me what the matter was, but I told them to leave me alone. Even Ray sounded worried, knocking on my door and asking to be let in.

"Go away!" was my answer.

I finally roused myself and went down to dinner. Everyone peppered me with questions again. I just mumbled, "I had a fight with Bobby," and left it at that. And I made it clear that I wouldn't answer any more questions.

So, we all ate in silence. I wanted to laugh, the horrible kind of laugh when you feel very bad but you laugh anyway at how terrible and crazy life is. The rest of my family tried to pretend everything was normal, whatever normal is. They talked about the weather. They talked about the controversy surrounding the merging of the churches in town, since the protests have started up again. And they ended up talking to Ray about his friendship with Roberta. He told them about a project he and Roberta were working on at school and a school outing they were going to go on. He sounded like he couldn't be happier. So nice for him. So nice for my family to sit there, pretending everything was fine in this world and ignoring me.

*

"It's scary how easily hate can come into your life."

"Yes, isn't it?"

"I can't believe I said those things to Bobby. I can't believe he said those things to me."

I was with Mr. Aniso in Joe's. After everything that just happened with Bobby, he was the one person I wanted to talk to. So, I texted him. Told him I wanted to show him the new Joe's and to talk to him about something. Glad he answered "Sure," as he always does.

We spent about a minute complimenting Joe on his new pizzeria, getting our slices, and sitting down. I couldn't wait to talk about what happened with Bobby.

"But—but how could we say those things to one another?" I blubbered. "It's so horrible!"

Mr. Aniso was nodding, looking at me with sympathy in his eyes.

"Don't be so hard on yourself, RV," he said.

I wasn't listening. "But don't you agree? It's so horrible. And so wrong!"

"And yet it happened, didn't it?" Mr. Aniso leaned back in his seat and looked at me. I felt like he was examining me to see what effect his words had on me.

"Yeah, it happened. That's why I'm upset. Bobby and I don't talk like that. Not to each other. I mean, calling me white boy. And my saying I could call him worse things. And then my saying 'fuck you,' like I hated him. I don't hate him. Do I? And he doesn't hate me. Does he?" I finally stopped blubbering and calmed down for a bit. "Where does that hate come from?"

"First of all, Bobby's had a serious injury," Mr. Aniso said. "Maybe it's coming from the injury."

"You mean it's not real?" I continued talking. "And what about me? Why did I say those things?"

The images of Bobby coughing and collapsing back on the sofa filled my head. "I thought I was going there to make things better, but my visit probably made things worse." I was about to cry when what Mr. Aniso said brought me up short.

"It's frightening what we can find in ourselves sometimes, isn't it?"

He was leaning back in his seat, examining me.

"But it shouldn't be there."

"But it is."

Mr. Aniso leaned forward again, resting his elbows on the table.

"That's the way we're built, RV," he said, his face close to mine.

"What do you mean that's the way we're built?"

"Like it or not, we have good and bad in us. All of us." He was talking very quietly, almost whispering. "That's why we all have to watch ourselves. Hate can come out and hit us between the eyes when we least expect it." He shook his head. "But don't keep beating yourself over it either, RV. Instead think about where the hate came from." He let go of my shoulder and leaned back, watching me again.

"It came from me," I answered.

"Yes. Why?"

"I don't know. I was mad. No. Seriously pissed off. I had come to do something nice for Bobby, and he lets loose on me. Says I'm lecturing him."

"Were you?"

"Well, I didn't think so." I thought for a second. "Bobby was acting so down and looked so helpless, I wanted to say something to help out. So, I said we've got to try to keep going even when life stinks." I realized I had been looking down at the table, so I looked up again and said to Mr. Aniso, "I thought of you at that moment."

"Me?"

"Yeah. When I visited you in the hospital that first time, you looked—you looked so bad. But you still kept trying to make me feel better. I guess that stuck with me."

"And you didn't think Bobby was trying?"

"I guess not. But what made him really upset was when I said I know what you're going through."

"I guess he thought you don't."

"No."

"Do you?"

"Well, not exactly. But—but I feel bad for him. I sympathize."

"Not the same thing, is it?"

"So, are you saying he had a right to call me names?"

"Not at all. I'm just trying to show you his point of view. How he heard what you said."

"But that still doesn't give him the right to act like a jerk."

"No, it doesn't. Remember, it might be coming from his injury. When the brain is affected like that..." He paused and then continued. "But even if it isn't. Think what it means for Bobby. Football is the most important thing in the world for him. Now it feels like it's been taken away. Pretty bum deal, isn't it?"

"Yeah, it is." I thought of the times I've been angry at God when life threw a curveball at me. I told Mr. Aniso about some of my conversations with the Big Guy.

Mr. Aniso smiled. "The Big Guy. Yeah. I remember that image. I told you, now I think of the Almighty as the Force. Not a person. But a loving force."

"What made you change how you think about God?"

"Good question. I'm not sure. Life, maybe."

We both sat there, deep in thought. Then Mr. Aniso looked back up at me and started talking about Bobby again. "RV, as I said, those things Bobby said weren't meant for you. Not really. They were meant for the injury. When we're really upset, we say things without thinking, letting the anger control us. Instead of us controlling the anger."

"Like when I said, 'fuck you,' and that I could call him worse things?"

"Yes. Scary, isn't it? Scary to think we have these angry feelings that can come out and control us."

"Those feelings are pretty deep."

"They are. And powerful."

"I still can't believe we said those things."

I became quiet, trying to process everything Mr. Aniso had told me.

"RV, you've hardly touched your pizza," he said after a while. "C'mon, eat. Before it gets cold. Oh, and one more thing, I bet Bobby feels as bad as you do about what he said."

"You think so?"

"I know so."

"I hope you're right."

I was glad Mr. Aniso was so confident. I wish I was. That anger coming from Bobby's eyes was so deep and frightening, I can't get it out of my mind.

After we talked some more, I came back home. I'm trying to do my homework, but it's almost impossible. Bobby's angry eyes are there, staring back at me wherever I look, whatever I think about. Even Mr. Aniso's confidence is not enough to make them go away.

Chapter Fourteen

Me, the Bad Guy

"Mark, could you please start reading *Commentarii de Bello Gallico* for us."

"Out loud?"

"Yes, out loud," Miss Wagstaff said, looking offended. "How else will you show us your knowledge of Julius Caesar's work?"

Mark began reading, stumbling over the words. *"Gal-lee-li-a est om-nis di-vi-sa in par-tes-tres, qua-rum nam in-in-co-co-lunt Bel-gae, a-li-am A-qui-tani, ter-tee-ter-ti-am-am qui ip-ip-so-rum lin-goo-gua Cel-tae, nostra Galli a-apple-an-tur."*

Miss Wagstaff was staring at him with those owl eyes behind the glasses. If her eyes could shoot lasers, I'm sure Miss Wagstaff would shoot them right at Mark's heart. Mark looked like he was breaking out into a cold sweat.

"Hmm. We're getting there, I suppose," Miss Wagstaff said, scrunching up her nose and turning away from Mark. I was happy that she took pity on him. But I was not happy when she turned to me.

"RV."

"Yes?"

"Please translate for us. What did that sentence say?"

"Um, Gaul is divided into three parts."

She interrupted me. "'Um'? I don't see any 'um' in that first sentence."

I cleared my throat and began again. "Gaul is divided into three parts. One is Belgium, the other is Aquitania, the third one is... Keltia?"

"Not quite," said Miss Wagstaff, scrunching up her nose again. "Quarum unam incolunt *Belgae* (there was the screech starting), aliam *Aquitani* (higher screech). *Tertiam qui ipsorum lingua Celtae, nostra Galli appellantur"* Well? *Well!"* (Full-blown screech.) Those laser eyes were fixed on me, and I was starting to break out into a cold sweat too.

But I was saved by Duffy. What? Yeah. Saved by Gangster Duffy, who's always in my Latin classes, but at least without his buddy Doyle this year.

As Miss Wagstaff's laser eyes were skewering me, I started hearing tittering behind me. The eyes suddenly shifted away from me. Miss Wagstaff lifted her head higher.

"Mr. Duffy? Do I hear you laughing?" she said. "What's so funny about Julius Caesar?" She looked around. A few people sitting around Duffy had been tittering also. She looked back at Duffy. "Well, Mr. Duffy? Or was that your friends making those noises?"

"No, no, Miss Wagstaff. We weren't laughing," a few people murmured.

Duffy raised his hand. "I do have a question, Miss Wagstaff."

"Yes?"

"About Julius Caesar," Duffy responded. He's amazing. His face looked totally serious now. I guess gangsters can do that—go from nice to frightening and back in a flash.

"Miss Wagstaff," Duffy was saying, all studious and scholarly looking. "I was looking up Julius Caesar online and it said, 'He was every woman's husband and every man's wife.' What does that mean?"

Besides scrunching up her nose, Miss Wagstaff also twisted her lips, looking like she'd just eaten the sourest lemon in the world.

"That has nothing to do with the wars in Gaul," she said abruptly.

"But it has to do with Caesar's life, right?" Duffy wasn't about to let go of this. "Doesn't it mean he screwed—I mean, he had sex with everybody?"

Miss Wagstaff's entire face was now scrunched up.

"So, were people in Rome all bisexual?" Duffy continued. "Can you tell us about their sex life?"

Finally, Miss Wagstaff had enough. She unscrunched her face. "We are *not* here to discuss Roman sex life!" she said, the screech starting again. "We are here to discuss Roman *history*. Julius Caesar's *writing is what is important*!"

Duffy didn't say anything after that and, after she calmed down, Miss Wagstaff went back to torturing me. How Duffy and his pal Doyle manage to stay just the right side of detention is another amazing thing about them. Scary, but amazing. Me? I get tortured for not knowing the exact translation of that sentence. Life just isn't fair. But didn't Bobby say that?

Our horrible last meeting is still often on my mind. But at least with everything I have to do in school, I can push it out of my mind once in a while. Term Two tests just ended, and I did okay. But Term Three is already zooming along and I'm feeling the pressure of that. Why, oh why did my genes give me nerves instead of muscles?

My discussion with Mr. Aniso is on my mind too. I'm still hoping Bobby and I can get over this, but I have no idea how. When we were leaving Joe's, Mr. Aniso told me to give it a little time. He didn't explain himself since he had to rush off somewhere. How much time? I wonder. And what happens after that?

At least there's Miss Sánchez to make me feel better. She's no pushover, but at least she's pretty to look at. Today she moved her chair from behind her desk and sat there with her legs crossed and her skirt hiked up above her knee. She's got pretty legs too. Long pretty legs. Is there anything about her that's not pretty? No. And not just pretty. Gorgeous. I saw Mark staring at her instead of paying attention to what she was saying. I bet most of the class was doing that. Even I was doing that.

Mark's expression changed when Miss Sánchez gave us back our tests from last week. I couldn't see Mark's score, but it was obvious he hadn't done well. I got an eighty-five. I'll take that.

After class ended, I could see Mark was feeling bad. We decided to get together after school. Funny, I seem to be the one now trying to cheer up my friends, who are depressed or worse. They all are. Bobby, of course. Carole. And now Mark. What does that mean? Am I such a paragon of mental health? Me? LOL. Good word, paragon. Means an emblem of something great. Like a beacon or a model of excellence you should follow. Boy, if I really am a model of excellence, the world is in worse shape than I thought.

Mark and I got a slice at Joe's and then went for a walk, ending up—where else?—on the rock in the woods. It's still winter, but Mark likes it as much as I do. When the sun shines it's really pretty, because with the bare trees you can see so far into the distance. And those hills I love looking at are always there, green or brown or whatever color they are at the moment.

And after I pointed them out, Mark agreed. He thanked me for bringing him to this spot, saying being there made him feel relaxed. Away from the pressures of life.

And those pressures are getting to him. As I suspected, he flunked the Spanish test. And flunked badly, getting a thirty.

I tried to explain that it was only one test, and it had been a pop quiz, most people didn't do that well. But Mark said he was struggling in some other classes too. And the more he was struggling, the more pressure he was feeling from his parents.

"Mom and Dad say there's only so much money for college," he told me. "If I don't get financial aid or a scholarship, I'll only be able to go to a shitty school, no matter what my grades are."

"Yeah, I have the same pressure," I said. "Money is on my parents' minds too. A lot."

"At least you're doing well. That helps."

"I'm doing okay enough. But I feel it will only take a few bad chemistry or math tests to bring my averages down. Way down."

We talked about the pressure for a while, wondering why the world had to be this way. Then Mark turned to me and asked, "RV. Do you have dreams?"

"I sure do!" I said. "Crazy dreams." I told him about Sigmund Freud's book that I got from Amazon and that I was reading to help figure myself out. "But it's not helping. Not yet anyway."

"Yeah, I had a crazy dream the other night," Mark said.

"Oh?" I was curious. Happy someone else was tortured by crazy dreams the same way I was. "What was the dream about?" I asked.

"Well, it took place in Spanish class."

"Aha!" I teased. "You were looking at Miss Sánchez's breasts! And she took off her blouse or something."

But Mark wasn't laughing. "No. Miss Sánchez was handing out a test, and she came up to my desk. But instead of smiling and trying to be encouraging, the way she always is even if we don't do so great, this time she was angry. She gave me my test, and said, 'Bad job, Mark. Very bad job.' And then she added, practically yelling, 'And stop looking at me! No looking at me until you improve!'"

Mark paused for a second, but he wasn't finished. "And this is what happened next." His voice trembled a little. "There was a guy sitting behind me. He hugged me, and it made me feel better. And then the guy said, 'You can look at me, Mark. It's okay. You can look at me.'" He was staring out into the distance, away from me. "That scared me. And I woke up."

Then he turned to me. "Do you think it's a gay dream, RV? Do you have dreams like that?"

I shrugged. "I have crazy dreams. Beats me what they mean. I'm just starting to read about them. They mean as much as if they were in Chinese."

"God, if I'm gay—" Mark burst out. He looked like he was about to cry.

"Do you think you might be?" I asked.

Mark looked as if the very idea terrified him. "No! No, I'm not."

"Who was the guy sitting behind you?" I asked Mark.

Mark shook his head. "I don't know."

He still looked terrified and I felt I had to calm him down.

"Look, one dream doesn't mean you're gay," I said. "And even if you are, so what? Besides, one dream could be about a lot of things. I'm not even sure I'm gay all the time either. I mean, I like Miss Sánchez too." I paused. *Though I really love Bobby*, I wanted to add, but I couldn't.

"You don't understand," Mark was saying. "If I'm gay, it will kill my parents. It's bad enough for them that my brother is gay. They're still not over it. And my father will never get over it. If I'm gay, too, I don't know. I can just see their faces."

I tried to sympathize. "Yeah, I know. I hate disappointing my parents. Why does that seem almost worse than having them angry at you? I haven't said anything to my parents yet about the being gay. It's too scary."

"Yeah." Mark nodded. "Being Pentecostals, my parents would feel like total failures. They'd probably wish they were dead. Or I was dead."

I whirled around, grabbed Mark's shoulder, and held it tightly, just like Mr. Aniso does to me.

"Don't ever say that!" I practically yelled. "Don't even think it! You're a good guy, and you deserve to live just like everybody else!"

I don't know where that came from, but I felt good saying it.

I don't know if I convinced Mark of anything this afternoon, but when we were leaving, he thanked me. Thanked me for being able to talk about his dream and his fears about his parents.

When we parted I gave him a hug, which he said was okay. I told him again not to let one dream bother him. And I added he could text me anytime he was feeling down or had questions about anything.

I gotta laugh. Here I was, acting like a paragon of mental health, giving advice about dreams and sexuality. I really should ask Joe if I could open an "office" in one of the booths in his pizzeria and charge fees. Who knows, maybe I could start a real business.

Hey, that's an idea. Funny how life works. Maybe Mr. Aniso is really rubbing off on me. He's helped me, and now I'm helping my friends. Well, trying to, anyway. Don't know how much success I'm having. Bobby said my attempts were lecturing. And Carole, I don't know what's up with her. I should call her up. And Mark, poor guy. He has one weird dream and he goes nuts. If he had the dreams I've had, he'd need serious therapy.

*

How did I become the bad guy in our family?

There we were at dinner, and Ray asked Dad if he had any new errands for him. For extra money, of course. Dad looked up briefly, raised his eyebrows as if he hadn't heard correctly, and then went back to his meal after a curt "*Ne.*" "No."

Mom and I raised our eyebrows too. Ray asking for work? He usually is the last person to volunteer for anything resembling work.

Ray wasn't giving up. He asked if he could shovel snow.

Dad shook his head, reminding him most of the little snow we had around here was already melted and we weren't likely to have any more this season.

Ray suggested cutting the grass.

Dad told him it was too early for grass cutting.

Ray asked about washing the car.

Dad looked up from his food again and gave Ray a hard stare. He asked him why this interest in being helpful all of a sudden.

Ray mumbled something about needing spending money to go out with Roberta.

That Ray. What an operator.

Dad reminded him he and I already get an allowance.

Then Dad remembered something. Yes, there was something Ray could do, he said. Cleaning out the garage. Weren't we supposed to throw out some old junk that was still there?

Ray said he threw out his junk. He said it was my junk that was still lying around in the garage.

Dad turned to me.

I shrugged, apologizing. Yes, it was my old stuff. I promised to do it soon.

That reminded Mom of some junk in the basement. Sure enough, that was my old stuff too. I hadn't gotten rid of those things either.

I tried to apologize again, saying I'd been really busy at school.

"*Mes visi esam busy,*" Dad said. "We're all busy." He said "bi-zzy" like he was making fun of it. He added that maybe he'd be too "bi-zzy" to give me my allowance this week.

That started a whole discussion about our allowance. Dad volunteered that it was about time he'd have to cut ours. Ray and I protested. Ray gets thirteen dollars and I get fifteen dollars a week, one dollar a week for each of our ages, which Mom and Dad heard somewhere that's what the average American family does.

Dad always thought it was too much, complaining about the extravagance of the American family, but so far, he hasn't stopped it. Now, though, he brought it up again, reminding us that his pay had been cut.

Ray suggested a compromise. His "compromise" was for Dad to cut my allowance by a few bucks and give that as a raise to Ray, since he was doing his chores—and volunteering for more. For a moment, Dad looked like he was considering the idea.

I wanted to kick Ray at the same time I was strangling him.

I swore up and down to Dad that I would find time to clean out the garage this weekend. And then I had to do the same to Mom about the basement, getting her to agree to wait for the following weekend for me to get that done.

As if that wasn't enough, what I call "Lith Time" is coming. Two, count 'em, two independence days, one in February and one in March. And the big crafts fair in March dedicated to that chaste patron saint of Lithuania, St. Casimir, who ruled in the Middle Ages doing crafts and other good deeds instead of thinking about sex. And sure enough, Lith Time is Volunteer Time. Just like at Christmas, Dad collects money and supplies for the orphans in the Old Country. Mom bakes cakes and does other things for the crafts fair. And Yours Truly helps them with all these things.

A discussion started about that. I've already told them I wasn't sure how much time I'd have to help with everything. Though after my last meeting with Bobby that might not be such a bad idea. But I held off. There are other ways I can keep myself occupied.

Good 'ol Ray suggested he could pitch in. And, of course, he added in his own saintly, St. Casimir way, if Dad could spare any extra allowance for all that help, he'd be happy to accept it.

Dad teased him about liking women with expensive tastes, but also said he'd be happy with the extra help, indicating that some extra allowance might be part of the deal. And then he gave me a quick look and shook his head, as if I'd done something wrong.

Even Mom got on my case. She pretended to be sympathetic, saying she understood how going to Latin School would keep me very busy. But she, too, shook her head sadly. She reminded me of Mrs. S-head, who shakes her beautiful blonde hair and asks why I cut myself off from the immigrant community every time we get together with her.

Is it such a bad thing for me to want to have more of my own life? Even a little bit? If they only knew everything that was going on with Bobby and school and all these questions whirling around in my head. And now, to top it off, Ray and I are switching positions in this crazy family. He's Saint Ray, and I'm what now? The Devil RV?

If they want me to be the bad guy, maybe I should try it. I've always tried so hard to be the opposite and look where it gets me. Well, maybe it's time for a change. I should really show them what being the bad guy is like.

*

I was lying on my bed moping. Yeah, I don't like myself when I mope, but let's face it, sometimes a person needs a good mope. Best way to vent when there's no one to vent to directly. I texted Mark, but he was at one of his fellowship meetings with his parents. Bobby's out of the picture. And Carole? I texted her too. But she didn't answer.

"Hey, RV."

What? Ray at my doorway? "What do you want?"

"I'm sorry," Ray said. "I didn't mean to get you into trouble. I'm sure Dad won't cut your allowance."

"Yeah. Sure." Ray didn't look that sorry. I even thought I caught a smile on his face.

"No really. If he does, I'll tell him I don't need your share."

I sat up in the bed. "Why are you being so nice to me all of a sudden?" I demanded.

Ray shrugged. "No reason. Do I need a reason?"

"Do you want something from me?"

"Hey, no fair." Ray walked over to the chair by my desk and sat down, facing me. "I've just been thinking, we could be nicer to each other. Besides, Roberta told me I should be nicer to you. She likes you."

Aha. Roberta again. Ray really must be mesmerized by her. Even in love?

Some of my anger was starting to melt away.

"Yeah, we could be closer. I've thought that for a long time," I said.

Ray was looking at me, not saying anything. "So, what's really bothering you?" he finally asked.

"What do you mean?"

"What's bothering you? You've been acting strange."

"Strange? How strange?"

"Just strange. Mopey. Like I used to be."

Boy. There really has been a switch. I laughed to myself. Ray the mature one, handing out advice. Me, the what? The problem child? The bad guy? But in a weird way, I liked it. Felt like a small burden was off my shoulders.

Ray was still looking at me. "I—I've had a lot on my mind," I said, suddenly needing to unburden myself a little more.

"Is it school?" Ray asked. "You? Mr. Genius."

"I'm no genius. But it's not school." I fell silent again.

"Then what?"

I told Ray about my fight with Bobby.

"You'll make up," Ray said. "If you're really friends, you'll find a way to make up."

"I hope you're right," I said. "But it's not just Bobby. It's my life."

"What about your life? You've got a good life. Getting As and Bs. Being praised by everyone. I'm the one who feels cheated, since I can never measure up to my amazing big brother."

For the first time, I got a sense of how Ray must feel compared to me. And I felt bad. "Sorry," I said. "I don't mean to lord anything over you."

"You don't have to. It just happens."

"I guess it does."

I looked down at the floor, thinking about something. I looked back up at Ray. "Ray, do you ever have dreams?" I asked. "I mean, crazy dreams?"

"You mean like cops and robbers. And being chased? Sure."

"Like that. And other stuff."

"What other stuff?"

I told him about dreaming about Bobby. And how I couldn't get him out of my mind. Even some of the romantic dreams.

"OMG, you might be queer?" Ray exclaimed.

"But I dream and think about women sometimes too," I quickly added. I told him about Miss Sánchez.

"But that's so cool!" Ray exclaimed again. "My perfect older brother might be gay! Or bi! That is so cool!"

"Don't tell Mom and Dad."

"Have you done anything?" Ray asked. His eyes were wide open. He looked like he was really enjoying this.

"What do you mean?"

"You know. Like making out or...or anything."

The memory of kissing Bobby came back vividly. And his hand on my hand and how electric that felt.

"A little," I said. "I've done a little." But I couldn't bring myself to tell Ray any details.

"That is so cool!" Ray kept repeating. "And I thought you were a nerdy virgin."

"I am a virgin!" By now, I could feel myself blushing.

"Okay, Okay. You're a virgin. But you're not a nerdy virgin. So, you get some points for that." Ray was really having a blast. I let it go. I didn't want to get into a discussion of what a virgin was.

"You're not going to tell Mom and Dad," I said again.

"No. Don't worry. Why would I tell them?" Ray stood up from his chair. "Well, I gotta go. Hang in there, Big Brother. If you need someone to talk to, I'm next door." He gave me a high five and left my room.

I sat on my bed in a little bit of a daze. So, I just told Ray my deepest secret. And he gave me a high five for it. What made me do it? Could I trust him not to say anything to Mom and Dad? But maybe it wouldn't be so bad. When unpleasant things happen, I often think it's the end of the world, but then things change so quickly, and the world looks fine. So maybe Mom and Dad knowing about me wouldn't be such a big deal after all. Images of Mom and especially Dad's reactions, good and bad, were swirling around in my head.

I still can't believe all this just happened. I told myself to get up off the bed and do some work for school. But sitting here with the computer staring at me, all I can think of is Ray's face staring at me. And the conversation we just had. Calm down, RV! Ray acted like it was no big deal, right? That's good, isn't it?

And admit it. It does feel good to unburden myself to a member of my family. I've wanted to get closer to Ray for a long time, right? I guess that's the way to do it. To open up to someone. You have to make yourself vulnerable in order to get closer to them. Now what happens? I don't want to think about it. I've got to relax first. Forget the Devil RV or the Bad Guy. I need a new model of behavior.

Chapter Fifteen

Pessimism to Optimism to Pessimism

It's the first day of spring, but it doesn't feel very springy. It's still cold and windy, and we had a little snow the day before. This shows that even though the world is supposed to be a certain way, it doesn't always follow what it's supposed to do.

Like people. Ray and me, for instance. So, I told Ray my biggest secret. But that hasn't changed anything. We're not suddenly bosom buddies. Ray sits there at most dinners ignoring everyone like always, paying attention to his cell phone whenever he can get away with it. If he's not doing that, he's badgering everyone about energy efficiency.

And me? I don't suddenly feel—what's the word everyone uses? Empowered. Yeah, empowered. What an annoying word. Everyone talks about how you should be empowered. Be yourself. Be strong. Show the world what you've got.

I've been trying to show the world what I've got for fifteen years. And what do I have to show for it? When I was pushed out of Mom and they slapped me the day I was born, Mom says I was yelling and crying so loudly they could hear me through the entire hospital. Poor kid. I probably had a sense of what was in store for me and wanted to climb right back into her womb. I didn't feel empowered then, and I don't feel empowered now. I feel like the same old RV.

When I try to show the world what I've got, I'm slapped right back for it. Like with Bobby. Except that wasn't a slap. That was a punch in the gut. A huge punch in the gut.

There I go, getting down on myself again. I know what Mr. Aniso would do. He'd put his hand on my shoulder, grab me tightly, and say, "Stop it!" Then he'd give me all the reasons why I'm doing fine. Okay. Okay. Let me try it.

I'm doing okay in Spanish class. And Latin class. And Mark and I are good friends now. And Joe's Pizza is doing well in its new location. And Ray and I started talking. Really talking. And Mom and Dad aren't arguing that much. That's because the demonstrations about the merging of the churches have stopped for the winter. Everything's on hold since people are waiting to see what the judge will say. They'll probably start arguing again when the judge rules one way or the other. So, until that happens let me enjoy the peace and quiet.

That reminds me. I haven't heard anything from the Big Guy in a while. Not that I've been praying or trying to pay attention to what He's telling me. So, I guess it's my fault as much as His.

Do you like that, Big Guy? I'm taking a little responsibility for myself so it's not all on your shoulders. Maybe that is another lesson. Okay, progress. Good. My new model of behavior.

So, when is it going to start feeling like spring?

*

I have to laugh at myself. Just when I finished that little conversation with the Big Guy about spring, guess who called? Carole.

"Hey! Great to hear from you, Carole! I've been worried about you."

Carole apologized to me for being so out of touch. "I needed time for myself," she said.

"Are you over that French guy, François?" I asked.

"Yes, I am," she answered. Then she giggled, that old giggle I recognized.

"What?"

"What?"

"You're giggling. That means you're thinking about something." I could just picture her blushing too.

"Oh, really?" Now, she sounded flirtatious.

"C'mon, Carole. What's going on?"

She giggled again. I was happy that the old Carole seemed to be back, and I wanted to know what was putting her in such a good mood.

She suggested going to Joe's where she would fill me in about what was happening in her life. "I haven't been to the new place yet," she said. "So, let's go there and we can talk."

I never say no to Joe's, so we went there after school. I was glad that Carole liked the place. And I was glad to see there were some customers I recognized from the old Joe's. Since the new Joe's wasn't as big as the old one, it almost seemed full.

"Business is good, huh?" I said to Joe, as he handed me my slice.

Joe gave me a thumbs-up. And he charged us half price for the two slices since he said Carole got a discount as a first-time visitor.

"He's a good businessman," Carole whispered, as we walked back with our slices and drinks to the one booth that was free. "That's why he's doing well."

Ah, right. The rules of business. I remembered the last time we talked Carole told me she and Tim had a big fight. I asked her what happened to the computer fix-it business.

"It's Tim's now," Carole said.

"No more consulting?"

"No more consulting."

"Did he give you any money?"

"Yes, he gave me two hundred and fifty dollars for it." Carole looked pensive. "I don't know if that was enough. But I was happy to take it. I was so depressed after the holidays, I just didn't want to deal with it anymore. Tim can have all our customers." She looked a little guilty. "I guess I owe you some of that money."

"Yeah, maybe," I said, not sure if I was upset she hadn't mentioned it to me before. But I told myself to think about that later. There were more important things going on.

"So, I'm glad to see you in a good mood," I said. "Thanks for calling."

Carole looked a little embarrassed, but she was giggling and smiling, too, so I knew it was a good kind of embarrassment.

"C'mon. What's going on? You know we don't have secrets from each other. We didn't used to, anyway."

Carole took a bite of her pizza and said, "I'm over François. But I'm becoming friendly with another French guy."

"What?"

"Yeah."

"You're kidding!"

"The world is crazy, isn't it?" she said. She was laughing. She looked up at me. "His name is Guillaume."

"Guillaume?"

"Yes. It means William in French."

I was sitting there with my mouth open, forgetting about eating for a moment. "Okay. I've got to process this. François. Guillaume. How did this all happen?"

"Well," Carole said, starting her explanation, "Guillaume is a friend of François. His family just moved to Boston. He called me because François gave him my number. At first, when I found out he was a friend of François, I wanted nothing to do with him. So, I put him off. But he called a second time, so I thought, why not? I'll be more careful this time."

She took a few bites of her pizza and then looked up at me, shaking her head. "By the way, we're not dating. This might just be a friendship instead of a romantic thing."

"What makes you say that?"

"Guillaume is nothing like François. François was handsome and confident and full of compliments." She giggled and blushed, the memory of François obviously still strong. "You can just imagine what it's like getting compliments in French all the time."

She took a sip of her drink and thought for a second. "Guillaume is so different. He's shy and fun in a quiet way. Instead of giving compliments, he asks questions. He wants to know all about the US."

"Sounds like a nice guy."

"Oh, he is."

I gave her one of my who-are-we-kidding looks. "Are you sure this is just a friendship?"

"Yes. No. I don't know. RV, let me just enjoy this without putting a label on it." Carole fixed her gaze on me. "And you, RV? What about you? Anyone special?"

I shook my head. "Nope."

"Are you sure? Why do you look so sad?"

"I do?"

"Yes."

My thoughts about Bobby were obviously showing on my face. I had to fess up, at least a little bit. So, I told her about my fight with Bobby.

"Wow, that's bad," she said. "And you haven't seen him since then?"

"No. I think about calling his parents to see how he's doing, but I'm scared." Trying to change the subject, I told her about my new friendship with Mark. "He comes from a repressive background, too, so we have a lot to talk about."

"Are you sure none of these friendships are romantic?" She was looking at me with a half-teasing and a half-serious expression. "C'mon, tell me the truth." She fixed that gaze on me again.

Ah, the truth. If we could tell the truth all the time without fearing the consequences, what would the world be like? When would I stop being held prisoner by my promise to Bobby that I wouldn't talk about us except as friends?

Carole started giggling again. "RV, I can see something's on your mind. And you're blushing. You know what that means? You're hiding something."

"No, it doesn't. You know I blush easily."

"Oh, RV. When are you going to be more open about yourself? You should see the people in France. They talk about sex much more openly."

I told her about my talk with Ray. "So that's progress, isn't it?"

"Okay. That's good," Carole said. "I'll give you good marks for that."

"No!" I laughed. "Not another report card! We get enough of them every term at school."

Carole started laughing too. "Yes. This is a sex report card. It's given out in life, not at school!"

We both continued laughing, finishing our slices and ordering two more. It was so good to have Carole back.

We sat there gossiping and trading stories for most of the afternoon. When we hugged each other and left for home, it was sunny and warm. I laughed at myself. Wasn't I just saying it didn't feel like spring? Does it simply take an old friend to be back in your life, to cheer you up and make you look at the world a little differently? Or does the world really change that fast?

*

Mr. Briggs is back in the news. He's the gay teacher who was fired from his school. The guy who Mr. Aniso and Ben were demonstrating about. Because of him I got a taste of what might be in store for me at home if I came out. And it wouldn't be good. None of it is good.

Mr. Briggs has been accused of having sex with a student in his class. By the student himself and his parents. He's a senior now, but he says when he was a sophomore, he and Mr. Briggs had an "inappropriate" relationship. The news didn't give details of what was inappropriate, but it doesn't matter, does it? The student was not sixteen years when the relationship happened, so if he's found guilty Mr. Briggs would go to jail.

All this was on the news when we were doing our family thing and watching TV after dinner last night. Mom and Dad shook their heads and said how bad it was that there were people taking advantage of children. I begged to differ about what constitutes a child, but I held my tongue. Instead, I said something about the teacher being innocent until proven guilty, and that Mr. Briggs has denied everything.

That comment went nowhere. Dad made a dismissive comment about so many scumbag politicians denying wrongdoing until they finally are forced to confess later. And Mom said the charges were serious enough that Mr. Briggs should definitely be kept away from the school if not in jail.

Ray, as usual, had a different take on things. He said the student was fifteen years old, almost sixteen, so what was the big deal?

"What's the big deal?" Dad responded in English. "I tell you what is big deal!" His eyes were flashing anger and his whole body tensed up. One of those Dad moments that always make us want to run out of the room if not the house.

Dad proceeded to tell a story I had never heard before. How when he was new to this country and started working at his construction job, he became friends with a certain guy named Lou. Lou was another construction guy, a little older than Dad, and he was very nice to Dad. He gave him information on how things worked in this country, where to get good deals on things, and tips in general on how to get by. Dad was very grateful to this guy and offered to buy him a beer one time. At the bar they started talking about their lives. Lou told him he wasn't married and confessed how lonely he felt at times. And that's when Dad said he got a "funny" feeling about the guy.

And then he said, "*Aš maniau kad jis mano tikras draugas. O ne išdavikas! Norėjo tik vieno dalyko!*" "To think I trusted him and thought he was a real friend. Not someone who just wanted one thing!" Dad shivered and shook his head as if he was warding off a slimy creature or a virus.

Dad wasn't finished with his story. He said Lou still tried to be friendly with him, but Dad told us he kept his distance after that. He said he wasn't alone in his fear. Rumors about Lou being "different" started going around. Then the rumors turned into something worse. Another guy who worked there said Lou made a pass at him. That did it. A group of guys confronted Lou one day after work and beat him up. They beat him so badly he ended up in the hospital and never worked there again.

"That's terrible," Ray said.

Ray's comment made Dad even angrier. His eyes flashing, he said if Lou had made a pass at him— *thwack!*—he would have done the same thing. He made a fist and slammed it into the open palm of his other hand. *Thwack!* Dad did it a second time. The sound was sharp and loud. And frightening, echoing in my ears.

"*Jam to reikėjo!*" "That's what he deserved!" Dad was saying. He added that men like Mr. Briggs, who betrayed their friends, deserved to be put away and punished.

Betrayed. So that's how Dad felt. And slamming his fist into his other hand emphasized it.

Even Mom added her two cents, making a negative comment about gay teachers. She asked us boys how we would feel if a teacher made a pass at us.

We agreed that it wouldn't be good. Ray said he would fight back and kick his ass. I wondered how I would fight back.

Ray was about to say something but stopped himself. I'm sure he was going to say something about me.

Maybe indirectly, like "what if one of your kids was gay?" But that still would have been too close for comfort. I even flashed him my own angry look to keep him quiet. I'm just so glad he didn't go there.

Finally, the newscast turned to other topics and we stopped talking about the matter. I was depressed going back up to my room. So much for Mom and Dad being supportive of gays. And Dad—forget it.

"They're just uptight," Ray said when he stopped by my room. "Ignore them."

"How can I ignore them? They're my parents," I answered.

"I still wouldn't say anything to them about you maybe being queer," he cautioned. "Not if you don't want to bring more crap into this crazy family."

Well, at least I'm glad he doesn't think bringing up the topic is a good idea. Not in our family. I just hope he doesn't change his mind.

Chapter Sixteen

Apology

My cell phone rang. I tried to act cool, but my heart started beating fast as soon as I saw the number.

"Hi, Bobby."

"Hi, RV."

"How—how are you?"

"Better."

"That's good to hear."

"I'll live." Bobby let out a little sigh. "I think."

"Of course."

"Yeah."

Neither of us said anything. I hate these awkward pauses, especially with someone like Bobby, but I just didn't know what to say, since he still seemed down. And because I still felt bad about what we said to each other the last time we met.

"RV, I called, ah, to apologize," Bobby said haltingly. "About some of the things I said when you were last here. I'm sorry."

"Ah, thanks," I said. "I want to apologize for what I said too. I know I came on like a bit of a know-it-all."

"No. You were just trying to do something nice. And I— And I...I don't know where I was."

"You were hurting."

"That's no excuse."

"I was so upset at what we both said to each other. It was—"

"It was bad," Bobby interrupted me, not letting me finish. Then he paused again. "RV. If you have any time in the next few days to come by, I'd—I'd like to see you and apologize in person. I'm still stuck at home. Though I hope the doctors will let me get out of the house soon."

"Sure. It's spring. I bet you can't wait to get a little fresh air."

So, we agreed. I'm seeing Bobby tomorrow. I felt a huge sense of relief as soon as I put down my phone.

But then I reminded myself not to get too excited. Yes, it was great to get Bobby's phone call. But does it mean things are back to normal, whatever normal is? That's an open question. I have to take things one step at a time.

*

Trying to still play it cool, I wasn't going to take anything to Bobby's house on this visit. But at the last minute I couldn't help it and stopped by Joe's. Getting a pizza for Bobby from Joe might not guarantee that things were totally back to normal, but I convinced myself it was a step in the right direction. Besides, it would make up for the pizza we never had together the time before.

"I need another recovery pizza," I told Joe. "Any vegetable surprises today?" I love teasing Joe.

He winked at me. "I have just the thing for you!" He went over to the glass case and showed me a slice with a lot of green and other colors on it. "How about my Broccoli, Cauliflower, Carrot Surprise?"

"What's the surprise?" I asked.

"You'll see." Joe put his fingers together and touched them to his lips. "*Delizioso!*"

Joe went to work. "I'll make you a fresh pie," he called out. "Give me about fifteen minutes."

I reminded him to give me two slices too–of plain old pepperoni.

"RV! You have to learn to try things! Life is adventure!" Joe shook his head. But he was smiling. He continued making the pizza, throwing what looked like a zillion vegetables on the dough. After putting the whole pie in the oven, he took a few pepperoni slices out from behind the glass counter, threw them on another pizza, and put two slices in the oven too.

Waiting for the pizza, I told him about Bobby's phone call.

"Happy to hear he is recovering," Joe said. He frowned. "But I thought that's what you told me last time. This is taking long, no?"

"Bobby's injury was serious," I told Joe, tapping the side of my head. "To the brain. He had an operation."

Joe shook his head. "Not *bene*. Not *bene* at all."

"No. Not *bene*," I agreed.

The pizza was done. I paid Joe, he prepared a nice package for me with the pizza, my slice, and two Cokes, and handed it all to me. "Have faith, RV," he said. "Bobby will recover. Have faith."

"I do," I replied. "I do."

I made my way to Bobby's house, alternating between feeling good and nervous. It was a positive sign that he called, but what kind of mood would he be in today? I didn't think I could take another fight like the last one.

It was Bobby who opened the front door. He was thinner. His face had a drawn, elongated expression. The bandages were gone, but the hair around that side of his head was shaved.

But he's dressed and opening the door himself, not lying on the sofa in his pajamas, I told myself.

"Hey, RV."

"Hey."

I handed him the package. "Some more pizza for everyone. And good wishes from Joe."

"You'll spoil us with these pizza deliveries," Bobby said, taking the pizza from me. Walking slowly, he brought the package into the kitchen.

He put the pizza on the table. "Unfortunately, I can't have any," he said, turning to me.

"Why not? You love vegetables."

"A lot of things don't agree with me these days. I think it's because of the medicines I'm taking."

"Oh."

We started to go to his room when his mother appeared.

"Hello, RV," she said. "Nice to see the patient up and around, isn't it?"

"Yes, it is," I agreed.

"We just have to fatten him up a little, don't we? Unfortunately, we can't do it with pizza these days." She told me the same thing Bobby had, that many foods didn't agree with him.

"So, we improvise," Mrs. Marshall said, trying to smile. But I could see the strain behind it. She was trying to stay positive, and I reminded myself to do the same. I smiled back at her. We were both probably thinking the same thing. We were happy he was making some progress, but he was certainly far from his old self.

Mrs. Marshall told us she would heat up the pizza for me and make something else for Bobby. She asked us to let her know when we were ready to eat. Meanwhile, she'd give us as much time as we wanted to catch up.

I started to go up the stairs to Bobby's room, but he stopped me, reminding me his bedroom was now where the study used to be.

"No stairs for me yet," he said.

I just nodded, noticing again how slowly Bobby was walking. And I noticed something else. His right foot made a little twitching motion every time he lifted it. I looked away as quickly as I could. Yes, Bobby was better, but it was just as obvious he still had a long way to go.

Bobby sat down on the sofa. "It's not as comfortable as my bedroom, but it will do for now," he said, seeing me looking around. I noticed a few things I hadn't paid attention to the first time. A chair had been moved from his bedroom. And another side table. But the football posters and trophies were still nowhere to be seen.

Bobby had propped himself up on a few big pillows to make himself more comfortable. I sat down in the chair facing him. There we were, sitting and staring at each other, feeling awkward again.

"Thanks for coming," Bobby finally said. "Like I said, I wanted to apologize in person."

"I wanted to apologize too," I answered. "I guess we both said shitty things."

"Yeah."

"Yeah."

We both stared at each other again.

"You look good," I mumbled, trying to say something to make him feel better.

Bobby made a face. "Don't lie. I look terrible."

I wasn't sure how to respond. "I'm sure it's been hard," I finally said.

"It's been hell," Bobby whispered.

I looked over at the nightstand in the corner. It was still covered with various prescription pill bottles, maybe even more than before.

I turned back to Bobby. "Any idea when you can go back to school?"

"No," Bobby said matter-of-factly. "Right now, I spend my time seeing doctors."

"Oh."

Bobby picked up a book. "I can't even read." As if to prove his point, he opened it to a page and tried to focus and refocus his eyes. He snapped the book shut with one hand. "My eyes. We need to work on them too."

"I thought they said they saved the optic nerve," I blurted out before I could stop myself.

"They saved it, but there's residual cognitive damage." He suddenly laughed, one of those laughs that's more frightening and angry than anything else. "I love all these terms. Residual cognitive damage. Like what the generals say when they're talking about dead civilians.

Collateral damage. They saved my optic nerve, but my eyes are collateral damage. Sometimes things look so blurry and I just want to close my eyes and not open them again!"

"I told you. I don't mind reading to you," I said, not wanting to accept what he was saying. I had a bright idea. "Maybe a book about football. I could learn something too."

"And I told you, I'm finished with football."

"Please don't say that."

"I am saying it," he repeated more firmly. Then he turned away from me. When he finally looked back up, he was shaking his head. "Take a good look at me, RV. Forget my head. Look at my body. My arms. My legs. I saw you looking at my foot. Yeah, where's that twitch coming from? And where's the muscle tone? Even if I went back to the gym, what are my skills like? You can't get skills from a book. You need practice. A lot of practice. How long would it take me to get them back? If I can't play contact sports for the rest of the year—if not forever—how long will it take me to develop any skills worth a damn!"

I went over and sat next to him. "Bobby, please! Don't talk like that!"

"Why? It's reality."

"You're already improving."

"Sure. So, I can limp around the house for a half hour before I get tired again? So, I take five pills instead of ten?"

"It's a start."

"A start of what? Not to play football? Probably not to play any worthwhile sports ever?"

"But—but—"

"But what? I'm still alive? Fifty, sixty, seventy years of this kind of life? It's not the life I want. And it's all my own fault."

"Your fault?"

"Yes."

"No, it's not."

"It is." Bobby started shaking his head. "I tried, RV. I tried." He turned to me. "But I tried too hard. *I tried too hard*!" He turned away again, so I wouldn't see his face. But I heard him choke up as he started crying, quietly at first, and then more deeply, as heavy sobs, the kind without tears, started coming from way down in his chest.

He turned back around and grabbed me, hugging me tightly, burying his head in my shoulder. The sobs were so deep, it sounded like he was trying to catch his breath but couldn't. "Oh, RV. My life. I just want my life back!" he managed to say between sobs. "I just want my own life!"

He continued sobbing, not letting go of me. The tears were coming now, wetting my shirt. I couldn't do or say anything. I just kept hugging him back as tightly as he was hugging me.

He finally let go and turned away from me. "I'm sorry. I'm sorry! I'm sorry for everything!" he was saying between sobs. "I'm sorry. I'm fucking sorry!"

"*No*! Don't be sorry! You'll get your life back!" I found myself yelling. Then I grabbed him and hugged him again as tightly as I've ever hugged anyone. "Don't be sorry, Bobby. Don't be sorry. Please don't be sorry."

*

I don't know how long we stayed in that position, hugging and crying, saying only "Sorry," and "Don't be sorry," over and over again. I was crying, too, scared for Bobby, scared for both of us, yet determined not to let go of him until I thought he was a little better.

Finally, little by little, we both stopped crying. Bobby's deep breaths on my shoulder became shallower and softer. But we still held each other tightly, not budging, as if moving even an inch would suddenly destroy the new deep bond that had sprung up between us. Slowly, Bobby relaxed, and I relaxed too.

Then Bobby did something that I'm still trying to process. He pushed away from me a little, grabbed my shoulders, and stared into my face. There was something in his eyes I'd never seen before. I couldn't tell if the look was angry, determined, scared, or a mix of all three. But it was so powerful I couldn't say anything. I could hardly breathe.

Bobby leaned forward, jerked my shoulders forward, and kissed me on the lips. Hard. So hard, it almost hurt. And he held his lips there, not letting go. My eyes were closed, and I felt numb, trying to process what was going on. I was more scared and confused than anything else.

Slowly, I felt Bobby pull away. I opened my eyes. He was still staring at me with that same expression. I stared back at him, trying not to show what was going on inside me. Not that I had a clear idea what it was anyway.

Suddenly it was as if we both woke up from some kind of stupor.

"I guess we should go down to the kitchen," Bobby said, his gaze shifting away from me. "The pizza's waiting for you?"

I nodded. "Yeah. What are you going to eat?" I asked, feeling sad that he couldn't enjoy Joe's surprise.

"Something bland. We're still experimenting with what foods my stomach can take. All these pills have really screwed up my system." Bobby looked at me and actually smiled a little. "Hey, don't look so guilty. It's not your fault. Besides, Mom's a genius when it comes to cooking. She can make all sorts of bland dishes edible."

His mother was waiting for us when we got to the kitchen. "There you are, boys. I was wondering what was taking so long." We sat down while she went to the oven and took out the pizza. She put a bowl of something mushy on the table in front of Bobby.

"Mmm, smells delicious," Bobby said. "RV said the pizza is some kind of surprise. Enjoy it, you guys." He looked down at his bowl. "What's my surprise, Mom?"

"It's a rice and chicken dish," Mrs. Marshall said. "With a few vegetables and lightly spiced not to upset your stomach."

Bobby turned to me. "It's amazing what you can do with chicken," he said. "I told you my Mom's a genius. I never knew I would be eating chicken so many different ways."

I didn't know whether he was kidding or not, but I was just happy to see him there at the table with me, eating.

Mrs. Marshall seemed happy eating with us, too, though I couldn't help but notice the glances she occasionally gave in Bobby's direction. She kept smiling, but I could see a few worried looks in those glances too. I figured she felt like I did. Happy to see Bobby looking happy and smiling but wondering how long it would last. I had been through a dramatic time with Bobby for about the last hour. She and Mr. Marshall have been through a dramatic time with Bobby for months.

Chapter Seventeen

Friend or Boyfriend?

We had a great time in the Spanish Club today. After all the stresses with school and worrying about Bobby, Spanish class is a place for fun. I'm good with languages and talking about Spanish food and travel lets me fantasize where I'm going to go in the future. Better than thinking about the present.

With the weather getting nicer, Miss Sánchez asked how many of us would like an outing to a Spanish restaurant in downtown Boston. Most of us raised our hands. I'd sure like one. A visit to a restaurant will make the experience real.

We looked at some restaurants online and chose a tapas place.

"*¿Qué significa tapas?*" asked Miss Sánchez. "What does tapas mean?"

"It means appetizers. Snacks on small plates," we said.

"Nombra algunas tapas."

We started listing some: *bacalao, boquerones, jamón, gambas, calamares, chorizo, croquetas, pulpo.* I know most of those, but then some of the kids who must have some Spanish ancestry in them mentioned *gildas, sesos, manitas de cerdo, morcilla, rabo de toro, criadillas de cerdo.* Don't think I'm up for those, but who knows? Anchovies and olives, brains, pigs' feet, pig's blood wrapped in intestine, bull's tail, pig testicles. I do love pork, but testicles? I suppose, though, if I told them about some of our Lith foods, these kids would be grossed out too.

Miss Sánchez handed out release forms for our parents to sign, and we left for the day.

"That will be fun, won't it?" I said to Mark, who was leaving with me. I laughed. "As long as we're not forced to eat everything!"

Mark wasn't laughing. "Hey! You're not scared of a little pig's blood, are you?" I nudged him.

Mark looks sad too often, and I've started making a game of trying to get him out of his funks. Some of the time I succeed. After my recent experience with Bobby, dealing with a person who's a little sad is nothing.

But this time it wasn't working. "Hey, what's the matter?" I asked.

"Sorry, I'm down," Mark apologized. "It's been a bad time."

"What happened?"

"My brother's disappeared."

"*What*?"

Mark said he'd tell me more later. We agreed to meet after school and go to our favorite place in the woods. We didn't stop at Joe's. Mark said he wasn't up for pizza or any other food for that matter.

"So, what happened to your brother?" I asked as we made our way on a path through the woods.

"Nothing. We don't know."

"What do you mean you don't know?"

"He's not answering my mother's calls. Or mine either. He's just disappeared."

"For how long?"

"Either Mom or I usually talk or text with him every few days. Now, it's almost two weeks."

"Wow." I thought for a second. "Maybe he's not feeling well and has been sick in bed."

Mark shook his head. "He would still be in touch."

"Did you guys have an argument or fight with him when you last talked?"

Mark shook his head again.

"Mom's getting frantic," he said. "She's ready to call the police. Even Dad's breaking down and talking about doing that."

Mark looked like he was about to cry.

"If something happened to him…" He stopped talking, lost in his thoughts. I gave him a small hug.

"It's okay, Mark. I'm sure there's a reasonable explanation." But even as I said those words, I felt nervous for him. How often do you hear a friend or a policeman say something like that in the movies and then the news doesn't turn out so good?

We ended up by the rock, and I suggested we take a break from walking. We climbed up on the rock and sat there, gazing around, not saying anything. Spring is really here. It's still pretty cool, but when you get the sun's rays directly on your face, they feel warm and strong. The trees are just about to get those little buds on their branches. And the hills in the distance should turn from brown to deep green soon. When I think about that, and feel the sunshine on my face, things don't seem so bad to me. The world is following the rhythms it's supposed to follow. If only people acted the same way.

"Do you remember we talked about prayer once?" Mark asked suddenly.

I nodded.

"Do you still believe in it?"

"I told you. I go back and forth about it."

"Still?"

"Yeah." I felt I had to explain myself a little bit. "I know that sounds so…so namby-pamby, but I guess that's how religion and I get along. Or don't. Remember I told you I used to call God the Big Guy?"

"You don't anymore?"

"I'm trying to spend more time thinking of God as a loving force, like Mr. Aniso does." I told Mark about our conversation. "Thinking like that I spend less time wondering whether God exists or not."

"Does it work?"

"Sometimes. Sometimes not."

"For me, thinking of God like a person helps me believe He's real," Mark said. "Someone who's loving and protects you." He was silent for a moment, thinking about something. Then he added, "At our fellowship meeting the other day, we prayed for my brother."

"That he'd be safe?"

"And that he'd come home."

Mark and I were both silent again. I was thinking that "coming home" meant more than just coming back to the house. But I didn't want to say anything.

"I hope the prayer session helps," I finally commented.

"Prayer works. I've seen it work." Mark sounded surprisingly confident. "As long as you pray for the right thing."

"How do you know what the right thing is then?"

"You know. Deep in your heart, you know," Mark said quietly, almost in a whisper. He was looking away from me, out at the trees and hills. Then he turned toward me. "RV, there's something I need to tell you. To confess."

"Confess?"

"Yeah." He looked away again. I could tell it was the same as some of those moments I've had. A lot. When you want to say something important about yourself, but you find it hard. So hard you often just keep quiet and don't say what you wanted to. And then you feel bad afterward.

I waited.

"It's about the dream I told you the last time we were together," Mark said finally.

"The dream?"

"The gay dream."

"Oh yeah."

"The guy in the dream sitting behind me in class. The guy who gave me a hug."

"Oh, yeah."

"It was you."

"Me?"

"Yeah."

We both sat there in silence again. And then Mark said, "I had another dream about you."

"Oh?"

"Yeah. You were in the fellowship group with me, praying for my brother. After the prayers, we all hugged, which we usually do. You and I hugged last. We hugged the longest." Mark stopped, looking down at his hands, which were clasped tightly together. Then he said, "One more thing happened. You kissed me."

I didn't know how to respond. Mark's hands were clasped even more tightly together. And he was just staring down at them.

Then he started shaking his head, as if trying to deny everything he had said. "I told you. If I'm gay, too, my parents won't be able to take it. I can't be gay. I just can't." He looked up at me. "You don't hate me, do you?"

"Hate you?"

"For saying that about being gay."

"No. I—I understand how you feel. At least a little bit." I told him about my father's story involving his friend Lou. Now I was the one shaking my head. "You should have seen the anger in my father's eyes."

"Yeah. There's a lot of anger out there."

I turned to Mark. "What about your religion?" I asked cautiously. "Doesn't it hate gay people too?"

Mark shook his head. "No, they don't hate anybody. They just think gay people are lost. Turned away from God."

"Isn't that almost the same thing as hating them?"

"They love them."

"But then they say they're bad."

Mark was quiet.

"I used to think like that," I said. "That's why I'm glad to spend time with Mr. Aniso. He's making me feel better about myself, and God, and a lot of other things. Maybe you should talk to him. I can introduce you."

"Does he pray?"

"I don't know, but I suspect he does."

"Tell him to pray for my brother."

*

Oh, man. After Bobby, and now Mark, I really need to talk to Mr. Aniso. I told Mark he's making me feel better about myself. He hasn't finished the job yet. I still have a looong way to go. But when I texted him earlier today about meeting at Joe's, he said he was out of town. With his partner Ben's family. There was a family emergency, and Mr. Aniso is helping Ben cope with things.

He asked me if I wanted him to call me tonight. I texted him back that I didn't. Told him I was fine, and just wanted to talk about a few things. But that I'd wait till he returned.

So here I am trying to be an adult. I can cope with my friends on my own. Promising myself to call Bobby soon. And seeing how Carole is doing with her new French friend.

I don't want to abandon Mark either. I feel really bad for him. On top of everything else, he's now dealing with those dreams that are frightening him. I wish Dr. Freud's book on dreams made more sense to me. All that talk of neuroses and sublimated feelings doesn't explain as much about what's happening to me as I hoped it would. I wish Freud were alive today so he could talk in modern terms.

And I can't believe Mark is starting to dream about me. Even kissing me. Wow! What if he does turn out to be gay and says he likes me? What am I going to tell him then? I don't think I like him. Not in that way.

I went down to dinner with a straight face, trying to forget my friends and all their problems for the time being. Those problems stay up in my room where it's private. My upstairs life and my downstairs life with my family, ha ha. I'm divided in so many different sections, pretty soon there will just be small pieces of me left.

I told Mom and Dad Term Three is going well, and after that there will be only a few weeks left. Soon, I'll be done with half of my Latin School career. Hard to believe, but I better not get ahead of myself.

Mom and Dad have been on good terms lately too. Though the issue about the churches merging and the new construction is starting up again. The judge will be ruling shortly, and the demonstrations against the construction have begun again with the nice weather. Luckily, Mom is busy with work and selling more jewelry online, so she hasn't gone back to the demonstrations. But if she does, well, let me not think about it now.

I thought I was in for a relaxed dinner, even with Ray's occasional badgering about finding more energy efficiencies in the house. Mom even made a special dish that Dad loves, *cepelinai*, which are potato-and-meat dumplings. I love them, too, but I wonder what the kids in my Spanish club would think of the added mounds of bacon and sour cream on top of the dumplings. I wonder what my arteries think of them.

When Mom handed Ray his plate, he shook his head, saying thanks but no thanks.

"*Kodėl?*" "Why?"

"I've become a vegetarian."

"*Ką?*" "What?"

Mom looked at him with her mouth open. Dad's face was scrunched into a frown. I looked up too. Just as surprised by Ray's comment.

Ray looked a little embarrassed but tried to explain himself. "*Jo esu vegetaras. Roberta irgi vegetarė.*" "Yes. I'm a vegetarian. Roberta is too."

"*Nuo kada?*" Mom demanded. "Since when?"

"*Nuo pereitos savaitės.*" "Since last week."

"*Ir man dabar pasakai?*" "And you're telling me now?"

"*Atsiprašau. Neturėjau progos.*" "Sorry, I didn't have a chance."

Mom gave him an exasperated look, asking if he expected her to make him separate meals.

Ray wasn't fazed, telling her he'd be happy eating bread and lettuce.

Dad was surprisingly silent, though I guess he could see Mom was doing a good job grilling Ray.

Mom threw up her hands and went back to her food. *"Gerai. Valgyk salotus ir duoną."* "Good. Eat salad and bread."

Dad did chime in with one comment. *"Pažiūrėsim kiek ilgam pasiliks vegetaras."* "We'll see how long he stays a vegetarian."

Mom and Dad have been so happy at Ray's amazing turnaround in being a good boy, they're reluctant to lay down too many rules for him. I wonder what they'd say to me if I told them the same thing.

And so, for the rest of the meal we had normal dinner conversation, talking about the news, more questions about school, and Mom and Dad sharing tidbits about their jobs.

Was I happy about it? Yes and no. Happy that we weren't squabbling. But still wondering how Mom and Dad would react if I did something out of the ordinary.

So, what happened to Bad Guy RV? Wasn't I supposed to turn over a new leaf in that direction a little while ago? Ha! That lasted what? About five seconds? I didn't even try hard, did I? As a matter of fact, I forgot all about it until just now.

Face it, RV. You're a good guy. You don't know *how* to be a bad guy. It's not in your genes. So when will you learn to accept what they did give you and forget about the puny muscles, bad coordination, weak eyesight, worrywuss nerves, frozen moments, crazy dreams, and so many questions you can't think straight half the time!

*

"RV, I'm inviting you to a party."

"It doesn't have a theme, does it?"

Carole laughed. "Nope. Just come as you are."

Well, I guess Carole is really back to her old self. Or even better than her old self. She called me to say she's throwing a party next weekend. When was the last time she did that?

I asked her what the occasion was.

"Oh, no big occasion. I just want to give Guillaume a chance to meet some more people."

Of course. Guillaume. I should have guessed it had to do with Guillaume. I wanted to ask her if they finally decided they were more than just friends, but I didn't dare. Why push it? I don't like it when Carole pushes me, do I?

So, I said I'd come. Wasn't busy next weekend. Ha ha. Let me check my busy schedule to make sure.

I did also want to ask her who else she was inviting but didn't want to go there either. I'm glad Carole feels confident enough to throw a party. I debated about asking her if I could bring Mark, since he's going through such a bad time. But I know Carole. She'd jump to conclusions. I can just hear her. "A friend? What kind of friend?" Wink, wink.

Oh, Mr. Aniso. I do hope your friend Ben sorts out his family emergency soon. Come back so we can talk about all these things at Joe's. As I said already, not on the phone. These things are not an emergency. They need to be discussed person to person. Preferably over a good slice of pizza.

*

I was happy for Carole. Since she's often complained that she doesn't know enough people, and she's been so down until recently, I was afraid she wouldn't have too big a guest list. Boy was I wrong! I got there a little early, and there were already about a dozen people sitting around in her living room, talking, munching on snacks, and listening to music.

Carole was standing next to a guy with curly dark hair. She came over as soon as she saw me.

"Hi, RV."

"Hey, nice party."

She smiled. "Thanks," she said and immediately brought me over to the curly-haired guy. "RV, this is Guillaume. Guillaume, meet RV. One of my best friends."

"Hello. Nice to meet you," Guillaume said.

"Nice to meet you, too," I said.

For a second, I wondered if Guillaume wanted us to kiss each other on our cheeks, the way the French do in the movies I've seen. But he just extended his hand to shake, which we did.

"I am so glad to finally meet you face to face." Guillaume smiled at me. "I have heard so many things about you from Carole."

I laughed. "Oh, oh."

Guillaume laughed too. "No, no. Only good things. Very good things."

I could see why women fall in love with French guys so easily. Guillaume's English was good, but that lilting accent he added to most of his words made him sound so sophisticated. Lilting, yes, that's the word. Don't know where I picked that up from, but that's how Guillaume's sentences sounded to me. Like the gentle rocking of waves picking you up and putting you down again, up and down, up and down. *Ooh la la!*

Guillaume and I chatted a bit more. Carole was standing next to him, and the more Guillaume spoke, the more broadly Carole smiled. If they weren't going out before, I was sure they're going out now. Even though she didn't say it, maybe this was Guillaume and Carole's coming out party. I'll have to tease her about it.

We agreed the three of us would get together soon so I could show Guillaume a few other places around town. Then he and Carole walked away to greet a few more people who came to the party. As the evening wore on, even more people came by. I recognized some of them from school, but many were strangers. I did hear that French accent from time to time, and it wasn't coming just from Guillaume. So, I figured he had some French friends in the city who Carole was meeting through him. Lucky

Carole. No wonder she looked so happy again. She could pretend to be in Paris while never leaving Boston!

I was standing by myself, drinking some punch, when someone tugged on my shirt sleeve. "Hi, RV."

I turned around.

Censulla, the smart gay guy from Latin class, was standing there, smiling at me.

"Oh, hi. How are you?"

"I'm just fine. Nice party."

"Yeah."

"How do you know Carole?" Censulla asked, looking around.

"We're friends from way back," I said. "How about you?"

"Carole is friends with someone who knows a friend of mine. You know how that is." He giggled. "And besides, Carole is in some of my classes."

"Yes. You and I are in the same Latin class with Miss Wagstaff."

"Oh, what a bore that woman is! Someone should take away her broomstick. And give her some laughing gas."

Censulla is a little guy, short and thin, but there's nothing small about him. He talks loudly, he moves his arms around like he's directing an orchestra, and he's definitely not shy. Even as he and I were talking, he said

"Hi" to a few people who walked by, making jokes and laughing before turning back to me.

"So, RV. How come I don't see you outside of Latin class. What do you do for fun?"

There was that question again. I told him a few things, trying not to lie, but also trying not to sound too boring either.

Censulla was shaking his long, black hair, telling me about his experiences as the new VP of the Gay-Straight Alliance at school. "What a pain to get people to participate in *anything*!" he exclaimed, his voice rising. "Are people afraid or just lazy?"

I shrugged, not knowing what to say. Why did I let people like Censulla intimidate me? He's gay and out there. Boy, is he out there!

"So, do you think you'd like to participate?"

Censulla was telling me about the Day of Silence coming up. Started in 1996 by students at the University of Virginia, it's a movement in schools for raising awareness about bullying and harassment of gay and transgender students. To participate, you have to take a vow of silence during the day in school. And you hand out talking cards, which tell other people what you're doing.

"So, can I sign you up?" Censulla was asking again.

"I-I'm not sure," I said, trying to get out of it. "I have to see what's going on that day."

"Oh, come on, RV. No one's gonna think you're gay just because you participate. As a matter of fact, you should come to our meetings. The club has been sleepy lately. We need to get things going. Maybe you can help with the website or bulletin. I hear you in Latin class. You're good with words."

"Gee, thanks," I said. "I'll think about it."

Censulla laughed but stamped his foot and shook his head at the same time. "No! That's what everyone says. Don't think about it. Do it!" Then he gave me a funny look. "We're not too queer for you, are we?"

I was so glad when Carole and Guillaume came by. Censulla started telling them about the Day of Silence.

"Of course!" Carole said, when Censulla asked her if she'd join. She turned to Guillaume and explained the concept to him. "Tell your friends back in France about it. This needs to go around the world."

Censulla was thanking her and pointing at me. "And make sure RV joins too." He turned to me. "We have to stop people like Duffy and his buddy Doyle from doing more damage to people." I wondered if he had any ideas about whether they were involved in the attack on Mr. Aniso last year.

"Have Duffy and Doyle called you names?" Censulla asked me.

"I don't think so. I stay clear of them."

"Why should you stay clear of them?" Censulla said. "They're the ones who should stay clear of us!"

Chapter Eighteen

Spring Is Springing

So now I'm an activist. I know I'll be doing it because Carole will hold me to it. It's something new for me, but I have to admit something. In a weird way, even though I'm a little nervous, I don't mind. It's the right thing to do. And as Censulla said at the party, it's not like I'll be announcing myself.

I told Ray about it after dinner when he came by my room.

"Cool!" he said. "I should do it in school too."

"Just make sure it comes out like legitimate protest and not acting out," I told him.

"Yes, Big Brother. I'll be good, Big Brother. You don't have to worry about me, Big Brother."

"I'm sorry. I didn't mean—"

Ray interrupted me, "It's okay, it's okay. Don't apologize. Everyone thinks of me as a troublemaker. I know the world is not fair. I can deal with it." He turned around and left.

I kept quiet. Maybe I shouldn't have said what I said, but Ray does have that reputation. There's a reason for it, and he's the reason. But I should be happy he's so different this year. So far. And I should encourage him.

I have other things to think about now though. Term Three finals are here. One more term to go sophomore year. I've done well enough this year (well, except for chemistry), so why am I still worried about tests? Is it really my character? Those lovely genes that determine so much? I am like Dad in a weird way. No matter how good things are, I'll find reasons to worry. There will be enough to worry about with junior year— ahem, Class II—coming up, with SATs and all that college stuff. Now, spring is springing. That should make everyone optimistic. Especially me, Mr. Nature, sitting on my rock and feeling all that optimism. Didn't I promise Carole and Guillaume to show them a good time? *A good time, RV! That's what you need to focus on. So, come on!*

What's that stupid commercial? "Don't Worry, Be Happy." I should take lessons from that. Wonder what people would say if they heard me whistling that in the school hallways.

*

I've called Bobby almost every day to see how he's doing. He seems okay, slowly, very slowly, getting better he tells me. And he doesn't seem bothered by my calls. We chat, but he hasn't been up for getting together. Today, though, he invited me over, which was a nice surprise.

"Hi, RV."

"Hey, Bobby! How are you today?"

"Not too bad."

"Any news about going back to school?"

"I'm not going back to school for the rest of the year," Bobby informed me.

"Oh?"

"The -ologists have told me I'm still not ready for it."

"The -ologists?"

"All my doctors." He let out another one of those half-angry laughs. "I'm seeing a therapist, a neurologist, a neuropsychologist, an ophthalmologist, a therapist, my primary care guy, the rehab nurses, technicians... You know, I never knew there were so many '-ologists' in the world. Anyway, they're the ones who decide my life these days. I'll be getting tutors. Hopefully, I'll be back to my old self by the end of the summer and come back for junior year."

"Okay. That makes sense."

I was glad he didn't say anything about football, and I didn't want to bring it up.

Bobby paused for a second and then asked, "RV, do you remember when you offered to read to me, and I put you off?"

"Yeah."

"Well, I'm sorry I did. I was just feeling so rotten and—"

I cut him off. "Bobby, didn't we agree no more apologies?"

"Okay, okay. Anyway, things can still look blurry, and I get headaches if I read too much, so can you do it for me? I'll be concentrating that way. You can be my audiobook. Hopefully you won't make my brain hurt too much."

I could almost hear the slight teasing in his voice, and it made me feel so good. "Or just come by so we can talk or play a game," Bobby added. "I've been cooped up in the house for too long, and I need company."

"Of course! I'm so glad to hear you say that, Bobby. It means you're really getting better."

"Yeah, I hope so."

"When do you want me to come by?"

He told me to come over whenever I had time. No surprise. I'm going over there later this weekend.

*

"Any news about your brother?"

I caught up with Mark after Spanish class.

He shook his head. "Nope."

"Sorry. He'll surface, I'm sure."

Mark didn't say anything.

I've always wondered about people saying things like that. They are being optimistic, though they really don't know one way or the other whether something is going to turn out well. And now I was doing it to Mark. Was it helpful? Or did it just sound patronizing to him. (Patronizing. My new ten-cent word. It means you act like someone's father, telling them things will work a certain way. But you're just pretending since you don't have a friggin' clue about it one way or the other. Yup, that's really how the world works. People being patronizing. And now me included.)

I tried to correct myself by telling Mark about the Day of Silence coming up. "Would you do it with me?" I asked.

Mark looked shocked.

"I ah—don't think so," he said.

"You sure? I feel a little nervous about it and would feel better if a friend did it with me. Carole will do it, but you're in more of my classes than Carole is."

Mark still shook his head.

"But it doesn't mean you're gay or anything," I told him. "And it is an important issue." Funny, here I was using the same arguments Censulla was using with me.

"I'll think about it," he finally said.

*

"Here you are, Guillaume," Mom was saying, ladling some soup into the bowl in front of Guillaume. "This is a traditional Lithuanian soup. *Barščiai.*"

"Oh, yes, borscht. We call it Polish soup in France."

"Yes, it's popular all over Eastern Europe and Russia. In summer, we make it cold. *Šaltibarščiai.* I like it even better!"

I can't believe I did it, but I invited Carole and Guillaume over for dinner. Even cajoled Mark into coming too. My spring spirit of optimism! Mom and Dad heartily agreed. They've been saying they wanted to meet more of my friends. So, they cajoled me into it. (Oh, yeah, cajoled, like you're getting poked, poked, poked. Not physically but mentally. As I said, Mom and Dad know how to do it really well. It's annoying any way you look at it, but it gets people to do things, I suppose.)

I agreed on one condition. No cabbage, and no foods that were too weird.

"So, soup is good?" Dad asked as everyone was eating. "More sour cream? Take sour cream!"

No one noticed the fingers of my left hand crossed under the table. And I prayed that Dad wouldn't say anything too dumb.

"I'll have some more sour cream," Carole said. "This is really delicious! I've never had borscht."

Guillaume turned to her. "*Mais non?* I have to take you back to France, Carole. You should see how we make it."

Carole was giggling. "I love the way Guillaume says 'Carole,'" she announced to everyone. "With that French rolling of the R. Cahr-rhole. Isn't it cute?"

Guillaume blushed a little, but everyone congratulated him on his English. I smiled. If Carole and Guillaume weren't going out before, they certainly had romantic feelings for each other now.

I glanced over at Mark. He was being pretty quiet, but he didn't seem too sad either. He said he enjoyed the soup and finished all of it.

Mom cleared away the dishes to make room for the main course. We all talked more about school and Guillaume's impressions of Boston and the USA. Of course, he was positive and said he was looking forward to visiting more places.

Then Mom brought over the main course: meatloaf and potatoes with some vegetables.

"*Zuikis*," she announced. "That's we what we call it in Lithuanian."

"We have the craziest names for food," I said. "Why is this called a rabbit?"

"It does sort of look like one," Mark said, pointing to its oblong shape. "And it's the right size. At least the main part of its body."

"No! You're spoiling my appetite!" Carole exclaimed. "Who wants to eat bunnies?"

"We call it *gateau de viande* in France," said Guillaume.

"*Gateau*. Cake. A cake of meat. That's much better!" Carole gave him a gentle nudge and said, "Thank you."

"Yes, *merci*." I laughed. "Everything does sound better in French."

The meatloaf was a success. For dessert, Mom served ice cream. No complaints there.

Mom suggested we all go to the living room to relax a little bit after the meal. She offered more soda and lemonade. And Dad kept quiet, not saying anything about vodka, like he had that time when Bobby came to dinner. I couldn't cross my fingers openly in the living room, so I said a silent little prayer to the Big Guy, thanking Him that the dinner was working out so well. Can't get away from those little prayers, can I?

We started chitchatting politely. Carole brought up the Day of Silence coming up. "We're all going to do it," she said.

I glanced over at Mark but couldn't gauge his reaction.

"Your teachers don't mind?" Mom asked.

"Oh, no," Carole responded. "Most of them are supportive. They know how important LGBTQ rights are."

Dad asked her what LGBTQ stood for. Just then the front door opened and in walked Ray with Roberta.

I introduced everyone.

"We were just talking about LGBTQ rights and the Day of Silence," Carole said.

"That's good," Roberta said. "We're doing it in school too."

"Yes, we're pan, so we feel it's important," Ray announced.

He got a few blank stares, especially from Mom and Dad.

"Pan. We're pansexual," Ray said. "We don't discriminate about sex."

Poor Mom and Dad looked like they were trying hard to keep it together. Dad couldn't help the frown taking over his face. As a matter of fact, he walked over to the liquor cabinet and poured himself some vodka.

"We'll talk about this later," Mom said to Ray, as politely as she could.

I glanced over at Mark again. He looked like he would have joined Dad in that drink if he'd been of legal age.

Luckily, Ray and Roberta left the living room, declining Mom's offer of having some dinner since they said they ate already. But Carole saved the day as she so often does. She started talking about some other places she and I could take Guillaume to. Everyone made suggestions, thinking of great places to explore, especially with summer not too far away.

And when everyone was ready to leave, it felt like the dinner had been a success. We can be a normal family at times. What family doesn't have their awkward moments discussing pansexuality?

*

I couldn't wait to go to see Bobby and was glad it was sooner rather than later. I thought about getting some football books out of the library for him, but then I remembered his reaction when I mentioned football. I lectured myself not to be too anxious and get ahead of myself. Told myself to let Bobby tell me what he wanted to do or what books he might want me to read from for him. It was a good sign that he wanted me to read to him in the first place. I shouldn't push things.

"Hey, RV," he said, opening the front door.

"Hey."

"What? No pizza?"

"It doesn't upset your stomach anymore?" I asked hopefully.

"Maybe not. But I'm trying to stay away from it." He patted his stomach. "Too easy to gain weight moping around the house." I didn't say anything but thought to myself that with Bobby still looking so skinny and frail, he could stand to gain a little weight.

This being Sunday afternoon, both his father and mother came out to greet me. His mother offered us some snacks as well as something to drink, so we sat around for a while talking. I was glad to see his parents seemed a little more relaxed too. Instead of glancing over at Bobby nervously every few seconds, they laughed and told jokes. A good sign.

Finally, the chitchatting was over. Bobby and I turned to each other.

"What do you want to do?" we both asked simultaneously. And we both shrugged at the same time too. "Not sure. What do *you* want to do?"

"Hey, guys. How about a movie?" Mr. Marshall asked.

"Great idea!" Mrs. Marshall agreed. "And maybe we can have a little dinner afterward. Can you stay for dinner, RV?"

I nodded and called my parents to let them know I'd be home later.

Mr. Marshall was rummaging around the DVDs on the shelf by the TV. "What are we in the mood for?" He held up a few DVDs, a comedy, a mystery, and a war movie.

"Oh, please. No shooting or banging. There's enough of that in real life," Mrs. Marshall said. She did glance at Bobby this time. "And I'm sure Bobby doesn't want that either."

"Mom, let me decide, please," Bobby said. "But no. I don't want a war movie."

Mr. Marshall started unwrapping a comedy from the DVD package. "This will do the trick," he announced to no one in particular. "This is really funny and will cheer Bobby up."

"Guys, let me make up my own mind. Show me the movie." Bobby made his father show it to him and then shook his head.

Mr. Marshall rummaged through some more DVDs. I noticed he was staying away from anything remotely football or sports related.

He took out a few more titles, but Bobby dismissed all of them. I could see Mr. Marshall getting tense. "Well, what do you want to watch, Bobby?"

Bobby shrugged. "I don't know. Something that's not stupid. Or irritating."

"It seems like everything is irritating tonight," Mr. Marshall mumbled as he went back to the DVDs.

"Yeah. Maybe we shouldn't watch anything. I'm tired." Bobby sounded irritated too.

I felt bad, trying to ignore the tension. But how could I? It was there on everyone's face. Did Bobby feel his parents were being overprotective? I guess I would feel that way, too, cooped up in the house with Mom and Dad for months.

Mrs. Marshall suggested Bobby rest and come back when dinner was ready. He agreed and left the room.

So, there I was, trying to make chitchat with Mr. and Mrs. Marshall. We talked about school and summer plans and things like that. I felt bad for both of Bobby's parents. They were trying so hard to keep me entertained and hide whatever worries they had about Bobby.

Maybe they were trying too hard. I could see how being with them every day for months could get wearying. And yet I couldn't blame Mr. and Mrs. Marshall for worrying about Bobby either.

It was time for dinner and Bobby came back out to the dining room. He looked a little sleepy. Mrs. Marshall asked him if he was up for dinner. He nodded. "Sure. Sorry, I was just a little tired before," Bobby said. "But I'm okay now." Mr. and Mrs. Marshall seemed relieved.

We all sat down at the table. Dinner was delicious, pasta with chicken. I was glad to see Bobby helping himself to food. He really has become so skinny. And he looked tired, too, even though he had just slept.

Everyone tried hard to chitchat again, but the tension was still there. I tried hard to make conversation, too, but there's only so much you can say about school, future plans, the weather, and whatever else people try to talk about when they're trying to avoid the real subjects underneath.

After dessert, I asked Bobby what he wanted to do. But he said he needed to rest again. I took the hint, noting it was time for me to go home, anyway. I thanked everybody, especially Mrs. Marshall for the food, and promised them I'd be back soon.

Progress. Bobby is making progress, I told myself as I rode my bike home, trying to focus on the good things, not the negative ones.

I thought back to my first dinner with the Marshalls last year when they seemed like a perfect family, especially when compared to my own. It made me sad, thinking about how much has changed and how much I've learned in the past year. The Marshalls are trying to be as good a family as they can, but they have their stuff, too, just like anybody. Maybe more, maybe less. With Bobby's injury, they've certainly had more than their share lately. They're trying hard, very hard, to get back to normality, but it will take work on everybody's part to get there.

Chapter Nineteen

Muchas Gracias!

I did it. I participated in the Day of Silence. Even though I made up my Talking Cards, I'm ashamed to say even yesterday I was still a little nervous about it and not sure I was going to do it. But something happened at the end of the school day yesterday that convinced me I just had to do it.

I was walking in the hall after my last class and saw McGrath walking ahead of me. He's the guy who got thrown against the lockers by Duffy and Doyle last year. He must have stayed out of their way this year because I haven't heard about his having any problems. And when I've noticed him in a class or in the hallways, he's seemed like another quiet guy, minding his own business, but okay. Doing what he's gotta do to get by, like the rest of us.

Well, yesterday that changed. As he rounded a corner to his locker, who came the other way but his old pals Duffy and Doyle. He stopped and Duffy and Doyle stopped too. Duffy and Doyle didn't say or do anything. They just stared at him with that smirk I know so well. I saw poor McGrath turn totally white in a flash. He just stood there, too, and I think I saw him tremble a little. Duffy and Doyle kept smirking, until finally they said something funny to each other and, laughing, went on their way. It took McGrath another minute or two to compose himself before unlocking his locker and doing what he came to do.

That did it! A small look like that can make a person tremble? No fair! I promised myself I wouldn't chicken out today. And, yeah, I've got to admit it. I said a little prayer to The Big Guy again. Sometimes you just can't listen. You have to ask! I asked Him to give me confidence. It's embarrassing to keep praying like this when I need something. I feel like a little kid doing it, but I do it anyway. And I wonder what The Big Guy thinks of when most of the prayers He gets from me are when I'm scared or in trouble.

I got to school this morning, and wouldn't you know it, my first class was Latin. And wouldn't you know that I was the first person Miss Wagstaff called on.

"RV." She pointed to me.

I stood up.

"So now that we're getting well-versed with Caesar's exploits in Gaul, what can you tell me about his *Commentarii de Bello Civili*? He's now in Rome, yes?" she continued when I didn't respond. "What happened in

Rome? We're talking about the Civil Wars now, right?" she kept prodding.

I stood there mute, grasping at the card in my pocket. Finally, I took it out and held it out in front for her.

She scrunched up her face in that way she has, looking at me with a puzzled expression. I moved forward a little bit, and she moved toward me. When we came together, she took the card. She read it.

"Well, that's very admirable, RV," she said, looking up. "I applaud your principles. But we can't forget our studies either. Since you can't speak, I need you to write in essay form what you no doubt would have told me. Five hundred words on the *Commentarii de Bello Civili*. Due Friday."

She handed me back the card. Then she called on Duffy. And I nearly fell out of my chair when he silently handed her a card too.

That hypocrite! Boy, does he know how to work the system and stay out of trouble. He'll be a politician someday, I'm sure. But at least he also has to write an essay.

Mark didn't stay silent, and I really can't blame him for that. He's got enough going on in his life. Enough kids did stay silent, though, that about half the class will be writing those essays. It made me feel good and gave me confidence for the rest of the school day.

I felt a clap on my shoulder as I was leaving class. It was Censulla, smiling at me. He mouthed the words "Good man!" and then went on his way.

The rest of the day went well too. Enough kids were taking part in the Day of Silence that I didn't feel like I particularly stuck out at all. I ran into Carole as we were leaving school and she asked me how it went. I gave her a thumbs-up.

She laughed. "Great, RV! You're an activist now, like it or not." Oops! She clapped a hand over her month to silence herself.

I felt good going home. There were still those little nervous voices around the edges of my brain, but they weren't too loud, and I could keep them from getting the better of my nerves. I really was happy that I participated in the Day of Silence. And I couldn't help it. I had to thank the Big Guy.

"Okay," I said to Him silently. "I'm not asking for anything today. I'm just saying I'm happy with myself. What I did. Being an activist. What else am I going to find out about myself? You sure do work in mysterious ways."

*

Well, dinner was lively at our house tonight. The legal decision came down about the merger of the churches in West Roxbury. The judge said they had the right to do it, so the group who tried to block it couldn't do so. Dad said it was the right decision. Mom said the fight wasn't finished. Ray asked Mom what her group would do next.

She said there was a meeting she planned to attend. They would discuss what action to take. She was hoping they would decide to appeal. She added that, of course, the demonstrations would continue.

Dad said he might join the demonstrations, but on the other side. He jokingly said he'd blow her a kiss from across the picket lines. He's obviously in a good mood. I guess the possibility of a better job is making him happier than I've seen in a while.

"It's going to be an interesting summer," Ray said.

The mention of summer made everyone turn to me.

"Nu, ka darysi šią vasarą, Arvydai?"

"Jau seniai laikas buvo apsispresti, Arvydai."

"Busi šešiolikos metų, Arvydai. Gali gauti rimtesnį darbą."

"Kolegijos ne pigu, Arvydai."

"Well, what are you going to do this summer, RV?"

"You already should have made up your mind, RV."

"You'll be sixteen years old, RV. You can get a more serious job."

"College isn't cheap, RV."

And on and on. I know I should have thought about this earlier, but with everything going on I just haven't wanted to deal with plans for the summer. Mom and Dad plied me with more questions. Mom looked at me with a pleading expression in her eyes, telling me she hoped I wasn't thinking of going back to Ed's Garage. Dad said if I didn't find anything else, I might be happy to be back at Ed's Garage.

They came up with more suggestions. Mom asked if school had any programs for summer jobs. Dad suggested I check out government websites and go to City Hall. Even Ray had a suggestion. He told us Roberta's older brother worked at MacDonald's downtown and loved it. "All those free Big Macs," he said. "Maybe you could bring some home. And fries too," he added. "Don't forget the fries. MacDonald's makes the best."

I managed to put everyone off, telling them I was looking into all the possibilities. "Let me get through the final term first," I wanted to say. I also wanted to ask why there was no chance of me having a low-key summer, reading my books, helping Bobby fully recover, and enjoying a little R & R at the beach or in the woods somewhere.

No, that's not in the cards for me. As Dad keeps reminding us, it's all about money in this country. And then there's college. Or should I say more accurately the cost of college. Never far from Mom and Dad's lips.

Fine, I get it. Let me make my own decision then. I'll figure out what I want to do. I just have to do it soon, don't I?

*

Leave it to Miss Sánchez to help me forget the pressures of life. We had our dinner out today as she promised. Actually, it was a lunch.

"The Spaniards used to have nice, long lunches," she told us. "Siesta didn't mean just sleeping but resting after that hearty lunch."

"They don't do it anymore?" someone asked.

"No. Things have changed. Fewer and fewer people are taking that nice, long lunch break. Modern life and air conditioning have caught up with them," she said sadly.

"That's good, no?" someone else asked.

"I suppose," she said. "But I like tradition. Our Spanish heritage. *Patrimonio.*"

There was that word again. Heritage. I guess it's important not just for Lithuanians.

Miss Sánchez brightened after she said that. She raised a glass, toasting everyone. "So, let's have a delicious, long, relaxing lunch. *Salud!*" Then she added, "*Arriba, abajo, al centro y adentro.*"

"What's that mean?"

"You'll learn in a few years, when you're of legal age to drink alcohol," she explained with a twinkle in her eye. "Let's order tapas!"

She had taken us to a tapas restaurant that had recently opened. It was a wide-open place with wooden chairs and tables and map of Spain on the far wall. Other scenes of Spain were along the other walls.

We opened our menus and tried to make sense of the food.

"Okay, guys. Do you remember everything we've learned?" Miss Sánchez asked.

"No."

"Yes."

"What's *revuelto de setas*?"

"Sounds revolting!"

"Hey! I know *pimientos*. Will they be too hot?"

"I'd like some *chorizo*. I know what that is."

"What are *mejillones*? Are they melons?"

We had fun trying to make sense of everything. I was glad Miss Sánchez was there to make sure we knew what we were ordering. Or to stop us if we were going to order something really crazy.

Miss Sánchez was having the most fun of all. And she looked prettier than she'd ever looked before. She was wearing a bright-green dress and a pretty red scarf around her shoulders that all the girls were complimenting. I could tell she was enjoying herself, laughing a lot, explaining things, trying different foods when they arrived at the table, urging us to taste this or that. The waiters enjoyed her being there too. I could tell, because they all came up to her over and over, flirting and laughing and asking if everything was *todo bien*.

I was glad Mark had decided to come to the lunch, too, though he told me there was no news about his brother.

"My parents contacted the police," he informed me before we had sat down.

"And?"

"And nothing," he said, shaking his head.

I felt bad for him. Finally, though, I saw him get into the spirit of things. It helped, I suppose, that he was sitting right next to Miss Sánchez. He started asking her questions and following her recommendations on what foods to try. I even saw him smile when he tried something he liked and thank Miss Sánchez for her recommendations.

"*Muchas gracias*," he kept saying and smiling at her. "*Muchas gracias*."

I laughed quietly to myself. Was he overdoing it just a little bit? I made a mental note to tease him about it later. It's okay to be mesmerized by someone, but do you have to try so hard to show it?

Then a thought occurred to me. What happened to Mark's dreams and fears about being gay? Had they disappeared? Or were they just temporarily gone in the presence of Miss Sánchez?

I looked at them again. Mark looked really happy listening to whatever Miss Sánchez was saying, focusing all his attention on her. Was he pushing himself to do that? Trying to push those memories of the gay dreams out of the way? It reminded me of my time with Carole. I did enjoy making out with her. But was I trying to push out thoughts of Bobby at the same time?

I got mad at myself. This wasn't the time to let my busy brain go into overdrive with all my questions. This was a time to have fun. There was Miss Aniso's advice again. One step at a time. Take one step at a time.

So, I raised my glass and made a toast. "*Muchas gracias* to Miss Sánchez!" I said. "*Muchas gracias!*"

"*Muchas gracias!*" echoed around the table. Mark raised his glass high, too, and said, "*Muchas gracias!*" louder than anyone.

Chapter Twenty

Good Things

I can't believe half of my Latin School career is almost over. It happened so fast. I didn't get any prizes the way I did last year. My attendance was still good, but my grades for math and especially chemistry did me in. I've been mostly on my own this spring. Carole's been preoccupied for most of the year, anyway, with other subjects like François, Tim, and Guillaume, ha ha. And lately Mark has been worrying about his brother, so I haven't wanted to bother him too much. That's okay. It feels good to do it all on your own. If I screwed up something—I never want to see another test tube as long as I live!—I know I just have myself to blame. LOL. This becoming an adult has its pluses and minuses, doesn't it?

We did have a special assembly to mark the end of the term. There was nothing as dramatic as Mr. Aniso appearing on the stage last year. This year, it was about climate change. Mr. Felucci appeared on stage and gave a talk about the project we began after the holidays, It Starts at Home. I felt a little guilty because I haven't gone to his meetings. But with Ray around, I feel like we've kept Mom and Dad in line. Even got them to make some changes, like getting better light bulbs and swearing off plastic. And I've certainly learned stuff from Ray. Nice to feel like I finally have a brother to share a few things with.

Mr. Felucci did announce a new prize—for the student who's done most to improve awareness about climate change. It went to Mary Henderson. I remembered her from the Halloween party when she went up on stage. She was the girl who had the Amazon rain forest on her head.

Her family stopped using plastic, changed all their light bulbs, bought a new furnace, and are even installing some solar panels this summer. Mary also got some stores in her neighborhood to work on changes. She's getting one thousand dollars for her efforts.

"Not bad," I said to Mark, who was sitting next to me in the assembly.

He nodded. "Yeah. Maybe we should get more active next year."

Carole came up to us after the assembly.

"I got a job for the summer!" she said beaming. "I'm working at Burger King downtown!"

"Hey, that's great!" Mark said. "I got a job at MacDonald's not too far from my house."

I congratulated both of them, trying to sound as enthusiastic as I could get. I still don't have any job. I even stopped by Ed's Garage last week. Ed said he would have been happy to hire me again, but since he hadn't heard from me, he ended up hiring someone else. It was nice to see Melissa, too, who was fully recovered from the gunshot wound she got last summer and greeted me with a big, fat bear hug.

I felt guilty about not going to see Ed earlier. And no surprise, I got a nice lecture from Dad about procrastinating when I told him Ed's Garage was not in the works this year. Like Dad never procrastinated. I wanted to remind him how long it took him to get his US citizenship last year, but I thought better of it. I'm just not as good at arguing with people as Ray is. I shouldn't dwell on my negative attributes. I do have some good ones, don't I?

But I did trudge home from the school, worrying about a summer job. I did apply to other places, but I haven't heard anything back. Not a good sign. I asked my guidance counselors. Even asked Mr. Marshall, but he doesn't have anything.

What am I going to do if I don't get a job? Volunteer work? I've looked into that too. Sure, I can probably get something, and still might, but it doesn't hurt to make a little money.

Am I becoming a money grubber? I hope not. I just know Mom and Dad can't give me a raise on my allowance. I'm lucky Dad didn't end up reducing mine like he threatened that time.

So, what will I be left with? Spending all my time helping Bobby catch up on his studies? Sounds wonderful in theory, doesn't it? But how much of me could Bobby stand? I doubt he'd want to see me twenty-four seven. He's stressed enough already being with his parents twenty-four seven.

*

Mr. Aniso called me. "RV. We need to celebrate the end of the school year," he said. "I'm not going to be around this summer, so I want to see you before I go."

"Oh?"

"I'll be with Ben. More accurately with his family in the Midwest," he explained.

He told me more about Ben's family emergency that kept him away from school earlier this year. He said Ben's brother was sick, which was a problem because Ben's elderly parents depended on his brother. Since Mr. Aniso is off for the summer, he volunteered to stay with Ben's parents in the Midwest until Ben's brother recovered, which happily he was doing.

"That's nice of you," I said, even though I knew I'd miss seeing him at Joe's.

As usual, it seemed like Mr. Aniso was reading my mind.

"But I don't want to go to Joe's," he said. "Oh, don't get me wrong. I like Joe's, too, but there's another place I discovered I'd like you to see."

"What's that?"

"Do you like Chinese food?"

"Sure. Most of it, anyway."

"I discovered a great little Chinese restaurant in downtown Boston. It's a little hole in the wall, but it's near the harbor, so it has a great view. And delicious, eclectic food."

"Eclectic?"

"Yes. Not just Chinese, but Japanese, Thai, Korean. They take those Asian cuisines and put the best parts together." He laughed. "I can hear the hesitation in your thinking."

"No, no. I'm listening."

"You've heard the term Asian Fusion? Forget it. That's too fancy. This is a mom-and-pop place that does things its own way. You'll love it."

I started laughing too. "Okay, okay. You have me convinced."

Mr. Aniso was still laughing. "Good. Ben and I love rounding out people's culinary appreciation."

There we go. It's not just Dad who wants to round out my skills. But with Mr. Aniso doing it, I hope the attempt will be more fun.

*

Good things do happen to me! Just as I was all set to give up on a summer job, I got one, which I immediately accepted.

The job is at one of the movie theatres downtown. I'll be an all-around gofer/helper/cleaner/ticket-taker/ticket-tearer/backpack-checker/little-old-lady-seat-finder and a bunch of other stuff. And the best part is I can see movies for free! Makes up for the crappy pay, but that's okay. I even went by to Ed's Garage again and told Ed and Melissa the good news, so they wouldn't feel bad about not hiring me. They both gave me big smiles and hugs.

Mom and Ray were pleased too. Ray asked me if I could sneak him and Roberta into the theatre if they wanted to see a particular movie. I laughed, asking him if he wanted to get me fired before I even started the job.

Dad was certainly happy that I'm working. But good ol' Dad had to ask what kind of movies they show there.

"Not crazy? Not sexy movies there?" he wanted to know, feeling like he needed to speak in English for some reason.

Oh, Dad. I was feeling so good, I gave him a friendly nudge instead of getting mad at him. "*Nesirūpink*! Stop worrying!" I parroted back his words. "Movies at this theatre are not crazy." I couldn't resist a little tease. "Maybe some of them will be sexy. What's wrong with sexy?"

Mom gave me a dirty look.

"You've gotta let me and Roberta in," Ray repeated. He got a dirty look from Mom for his pains.

What a great thing for the entire family when something, even a little thing, turns out well and we're all in a good mood together for a change.

Mr. Aniso congratulated me too. I met him at the Chinese restaurant, following the instructions he gave me on how to get there. The place was a hole in the wall as he had said, but the view over the water made it relaxing. And the food? I hope I didn't disappoint him when after looking over the confusing menu I ordered chicken chow mein. That is about as traditional and boring as you can get in a Chinese restaurant. No fusing any weird foods for me. Mr. Aniso didn't say anything, though, just offering for me to try his fancy dish when he picked it up at the counter.

I said I would. I told him between the Spanish tapas and the Lith food Mom serves and Joe's pizza, I felt my culinary appreciation was becoming quite international already. Enough for now anyway.

We lifted our Cokes and toasted each other to that statement.

It was so good being with Mr. Aniso. I don't see him that often anymore. He's given me so much, and I was having so much fun showing him I was doing okay.

We got our food. My chicken chow mein didn't look like any I've had before, with narrow yellow noodles and pungent spices. But it was okay. To be a good sport, I tried

Mr. Aniso's fishy soup dish. Whatever food was fused in there was not to my liking. Mr. Aniso laughed and said it was okay. That liking some international foods was an acquired skill.

"Good," I responded. "I'll wait to acquire it."

We both had a good laugh over that one. Then we settled down and got a little more serious as we ate our food.

We talked more about Ben and his family. I told him it was nice of him to give up part of his summer to help Ben's parents.

"That's what partners do for each other," he said. "Helping each other during tough times. It's one of the ingredients of a good relationship, isn't it?"

That led to talk about Bobby. Mr. Aniso asked me how he was doing. I told him about my last visit. "He's getting better, but very slowly." I said. "I think it will take longer than he'd like. Than any of us would like."

"I'm sure it will," Mr. Aniso agreed. "The poor guy has had a devasting injury." He gave me a pointed look. "I know from devastating injuries, don't I?"

I nodded and didn't say anything, wondering how long recovery was really going to take for Bobby. And what Bobby would have to go through to get back to his old self.

"RV." Mr. Aniso was looking at me with that serious teacher expression he sometimes has. "RV. Do me a favor?"

"Yes?"

"Be patient with Bobby. This injury has taken a lot from him. It may take him a long time to get some things back."

"I know. I was wondering the same thing."

"He's still angry," Mr. Aniso said. "I'm sure of it. Maybe not all the time, but I'm sure it's there." He reminded me of the story he told me about himself after he left the seminary. "Sometimes you know you shouldn't be angry, that you're just hurting yourself by—by doing certain things. But you can't help it. You need to be angry. And do angry things."

"You're scaring me a little," I confessed.

"Oh, I'm sorry. I didn't mean to. Why?"

"I get scared when Bobby gets angry. Angry at me, I mean. I just want to roll up into a little ball and disappear."

Mr. Aniso apologized. "I'm sorry," he repeated a few times, trying to explain himself. "I meant what I said in another way. I said it because I think you're strong enough."

"Me? Strong enough?"

"Yes. To understand that when Bobby gets angry, he's not really angry at you." He paused, and then added, "And to let it go."

I sat there silently, thinking about what Mr. Aniso was telling me. I know he's said it before, and it was meant in a positive way. But I'm not sure if he was giving me more credit than I deserved.

"One more thing," he said after a bit.

"What?"

"If you get scared or annoyed, remember, in the long run, you're helping Bobby."

"How?"

"Just by being there. Not abandoning him." Mr. Aniso gave me a searching look. "What have we been saying about relationships?"

"That people help one another during tough times?"

"Yes. You're building a stronger relationship with Bobby." He thought for a second. "Let me ask you something. Do you think Bobby abandoned you?"

I was going to say I thought he was, during much of the school year. But then I remembered the kiss he gave me that time after he broke down. What was he trying to tell me?

Mr. Aniso was looking at me. "Yes?" He smiled and twirled his finger in a little circle in front of my forehead, our signal that he knew a million questions were ricocheting around in that brain of mine.

I smiled too. "Just thinking about Bobby and me. Friendships can be complicated."

Mr. Aniso laughed. "You got that right." He turned serious again.

"After everything you and Bobby have been through this year, think how much stronger it will be. You believe that, don't you?"

"I guess so."

"Whatever happens in the future between you two, you'll always know you helped a friend through a very difficult time." He smiled. "Doesn't that make you feel good about friendships?"

"I guess, it does," I said. "Yeah. I guess, it does."

*

"Would you like to take a walk outside with me?"

"Oh, great! You're up for a walk?"

"Yeah. They let me out of the house now. And I don't need a leash."

I tried to ignore Bobby's joke, if that's what it was.

"Where should we walk? It's a gorgeous day."

"Just anywhere. Doesn't matter. As long as we're outside."

I was with Bobby. He had called me and seemed in a decent enough mood. The good news was that he's started to exercise a little bit and wants to get out of the house more. I know walking might seem like baby steps, but Bobby seemed pleased about it. "I know it's baby steps, but I have to start somewhere, don't I?" he said when we met.

We started walking down the streets in his neighborhood. I kept it slow, mindful of Bobby's energy level. And I couldn't help glancing down at his foot occasionally. I didn't see any twitching.

Something about a perfect summer day makes me feel so optimistic. Life doesn't get much better, does it? I tried not to talk about the optimism too much, though, keeping in mind what Mr. Aniso had said about what Bobby might be feeling. I glanced over at Bobby's face, too, as he held it up to the sun. His pleasure seemed genuine. No more jokes about being on a leash or being an invalid.

I asked him how the tutoring was coming along.

"It's okay," he said. "I have different tutors for different subjects. There's a schedule. I'm almost busier than I was in school." He laughed. "My English tutor sucks though. His name is Mr. Twiddlebaum. I call him Mr. Twiddledee. He's very skinny, has a squeaky voice and drives me crazy." Bobby mimicked him, increasing the pitch of his voice and talking very fast. "Bobby. What is your favorite scene in *The Adventures of Huckleberry Finn*? Why? Who are the protagonists and antagonists?" He turned to me. "Shit, man. I'm just trying to learn to read a few paragraphs without a headache or my eyesight getting all blurry. Give me a break!"

We laughed. "I want to ask the school if they could let you be my English instructor," he said. "But I don't think they'd go for that."

"No, they wouldn't."

Bobby nudged me playfully. "Aw, c'mon. You did say you wanted to read to me. Won't you support me in this?" He nudged me again, adding a little tickle. "You did get an A in English, right? Or was it an A-plus? I bet you could do a good BS job if you wanted to."

I hadn't seen Bobby so cheerful since last summer—when he told me about making the varsity team. The memory depressed me when I thought about what happened afterward.

"What's the matter?" Bobby asked.

"Oh, nothing." I realized the bad memory must be showing on my face. "I'm glad—I'm glad to see you doing so much better," I said, trying to change the subject quickly.

Bobby was nodding thoughtfully. "Yeah," he said. "I guess I am today."

"You really are." I wanted to reinforce it.

"There are good days and bad days," Bobby responded. "But I decided I want to live."

"That's good," I said, though the statement shocked me a little. Had Bobby really convinced himself this spring of the opposite?

He turned to me. As usual, my face must have been showing what I felt. "Don't be upset," he said. "I'm over moping and feeling sorry for myself. I'm going to get better. Better than before."

The old determination was back in his eyes, something I haven't seen in so long.

He smiled. "Let's enjoy today. Today is a good day." He gave me a little playful nudge with his shoulder. "Maybe because you're with me."

"Thanks," I said. "Hey, do you want to go and sit on our rock in the woods? It will remind us of the good things of summer."

Bobby shook his head. "Actually, do you mind coming back to the house with me? I'm a little tired."

"Oh, sure."

I tried not to let any disappointment show, reminding myself about the baby steps. "Maybe you can read a book to me," Bobby suggested. He smiled again. "And nothing with onomatopoeia, oxymorons, or paradoxes, please," he added.

I appreciated the gesture. "Okay, let's go."

We walked back to the house and went to Bobby's room.

Bobby lay down on the sofa bed. He took off his shoes and propped himself up with a couple of pillows. I looked through a stash of books on the side table.

"Do you think there are enough books there?" Bobby asked. "Mom and Dad bought them all."

"Hey, have you read *The Lord of the Rings?*" I asked, spying the first book of the trilogy on the side table.

"No."

"They made movies out of the books."

"I know them. But they're long. Start with something shorter."

"Okay. We'll start with *The Hobbit*," I said, seeing that book on the table too. "It's a good intro to Middle Earth."

"Middle Earth?"

"Yeah, you'll see. Besides hobbits, it's got wizards and dwarves and elves and trolls. My favorite character is Gollum, who lost his ring."

Bobby gave me a *whatever* expression but settled in to listen. I sat in the chair at the foot of the bed and began to read about Bilbo Baggins and his hobbit-hole.

"What? Who? How tall?" Bobby asked. "I can't hear you."

I saw his eyes were closed. "Maybe you need to rest. Maybe I should go and read another time," I suggested.

"No, no. I want to learn about what's his name. Here, come up on the bed beside me. And then read. It will be easier for me to hear."

"You sure?"

"I'm sure."

So, I took my shoes off, too, found a few more pillows to prop myself up with, and lay down next to Bobby. There wasn't much room, but we made it work.

I began reading about Bilbo Baggins again, one hand holding the open book, the other hand lying next to

Bobby. He closed his eyes again. "Keep going. I'm listening," he said. And he put his hand on top of mine.

And there we were, lying side by side, his hand on top of mine and me reading *The Hobbit* to him.

It's going to be a good summer. I have to believe it. It's going to be a good summer.

Acknowledgements

The author would like to thank Alex and Pilar for their help with the text.

About the Author

Andy V. Roamer grew up in the Boston area and moved to New York City after college. He worked in book publishing for many years, starting out in the children's and YA books division and then wearing many other hats. This is his third novel about RV, the teenage son of immigrants from Lithuania in Eastern Europe, as RV tries to navigate his demanding high school, his budding sexuality, and new relationships. He has written an adult novel, *Confessions of a Gay Curmudgeon*, under the pen name Andy V. Ambrose. To relax, Andy loves to ride his bike, read, watch foreign and independent movies, and travel.

Email
andyvroamer@gmail.com

Facebook
www.facebook.com/andyvroamer

Instagram
www.instagram.com/andy_v_roamer

Website
www.thepizzachronicles.com

Other NineStar books by this author

Why Can't Life Be Like Pizza?

Why Can't Freshman Summer Be Like Pizza?

Also Available from NineStar Press

Connect with NineStar Press

www.ninestarpress.com

www.facebook.com/ninestarpress

www.facebook.com/groups/NineStarNiche

www.twitter.com/ninestarpress

www.ingramcontent.com/pod-product-compliance
Lightning Source LLC
Chambersburg PA
CBHW020606110726
47899CB00002B/394